Forgotten Babylon

COLLECTOR'S EDITION

By Mia Vasquez

Many of the characters are influenced by Babylon and

Samarian myths and legends. All characters, events and

dialogue have been adapted in the process of dramatization

for an intriguing fictional tale.

Prologue

Before the world came to be, there existed gods who lived within "The Divine Garden". Each culture found a different name for it, but the name that graced the tongues of those that made this place was "Eden". A council was devised to oversee all of creation, and each god had their role to play. Those within the council were given titles and powers best suited to their skills. These rulers were named Anu, Urus, Ninsun, Enlil, Enki, Utu, Nanna, Tiamat, Marduk, and Nergal. Anu, the King of Gods, bathed everything in his heavenly glory, from the heavens themselves to the Earth below. As the Goddess of all creation, Anu's wife Urus cradled the world to her bosom and breathed life into it. Ninsun, their lovely daughter, had dominion over the herd and farm-like animals. Enlil is the God of Chaos, whose purpose was to oversee trouble and chance in the world. The brothers Utu and Nanna have power over the sun and moon respectively. Tiamat rules the sea and the life that dwells within it. Anu's brother Marduk was the God of War. Finally, Nergal oversaw the underworld and its inhabitants.

Chapter 1:

All throughout the garden, creatures called "fey" would frolic and dance. These creatures were gifted to the Goddess Urus, who decided upon seeing their beauty that they should live with her and her loved ones. As a consequence of their presence in the garden, Anu and Urus agreed to one day let them leave the garden and tread upon the world for both pleasure and service. Filled with gratitude, the fey vowed to please their rulers in whatever way they saw fit. This bond was not held with bitterness or silent contempt. Rather, most of them took pride in their duties. The youngest fey, Arwen, was one of these creatures that frolicked within the garden at her lord's behest. Her skin was as beautiful and pale as fresh snow, and her lips were so crimson that even the most prideful roses of the gardens could not help but blush. Her hair flowed like a calm river, and it ever so slightly graced the ground with its touch with every step she took. Upon inquiring about the strange purple color of her hair. Arwen would often simply bat her sapphire eyes at whoever asked and merely skipped away. To add to her beauty, Arwen and the other fey would often adorn themselves with the orange, red, white, and pink flowers; often to mimic the crowns that adorned the heads of those that watched over them.

Out of all the gifts that Anu had ever given his wife, Arwen was the one he was the proudest of. Anu had no intention of ever sending Arwen to the land of men; although, whether this was for her safety or for his queen's happiness he could not see. If Anu had his way, he would have her remain in the garden until the end of time. Here she could be happy and safe, and everyone could marvel at her beauty and overall loveliness. Anu could not fathom why Arwen might ever wish to leave. Every day, he watched Arwen dance among the tiny birds. She was most fond of the ones with beautiful teal bodies, especially the way they flew around her when she walked by. The little birds' wings flapped quickly enough that they emitted a strange humming sound as they flew by. As they took the nectar from the flowers, she thought for a moment and decided that hummingbirds were as good a name for them as any.

"Are the fey not lovely, my beloved?" Urus said as she placed her hand on Anu's shoulder. She smiled lovingly at her husband for a brief moment, then rested her head upon his chest as she gazed upon the fey. They danced and played among the flowers surrounding the terrace, celebrating another glorious day of life under the warm sun.

"Indeed, they are. Still, it troubles me that our daughter could not watch them grow alongside us." Anu murmured without even attempting to hide his discontentment. His eyes were filled with a quiet sort of sorrow as he looked onward, his gaze unable to match that of his queen.

"I miss her too but, at least Arwen keeps us company. If a tear should come to either of our eyes, you can trust that she will be upon us without even asking; doing everything within her power to ensure that we are right as rain."

She gave a knowing look towards her king and placed her hand upon his stubbled chin. She gently stroked it with her thumb for a moment before placing a sweet kiss upon his lips. With her eyes still closed, she nuzzled her smooth cheek against his; similar to how a lion might press against their mate.

"I know it is not the same nor will it ever be, but we should still be grateful for what we do have; and look to the future rather than fill our hearts with pain from the past." With a nod of begrudging of agreement and acceptance, Anu leaned his head back and tried to relax in the chair he was currently lounging in. With a pleased smile, the Goddess simply rested her head upon her husband's chest. She gently reached up and tucked her hair out of her face so she could look upon her garden. Her pale fingers slowly raked through her emerald locks, and she could not help but admire the red streaks laced all throughout her hair. As she placed a final kiss upon her king's chest, she pulled away from his embrace; she felt a small tug on her flowing white dress. Casting her gaze downward, she smiled sweetly at the beautiful Arwen as she looked down into those beautiful eyes of hers.

"Can you play with us today?" Arwen asked in her sweet, high-pitched voice. The two Gods were powerless to stop the warmth spread through their hearts as they looked upon the young child. Despite the previous conversation about their mutual ache over their absent daughter, this little fey brought joy and bliss to their faces without even trying. Furthermore, unlike the other fey, she dared to act without an order. Although she was free to do as she wished, she chose to stay and act as a light for the Things were peaceful within the garden, as they had always been. And yet, even here, such a thing was not meant to last.

Chapter 2:

Stepping through the field of flowers came their beloved child, Ninsun. She had finally come home, although the news she bore was less than magnificent. She had found a mate and bore a child, who she had elected to name Gilmos. A whirlwind of emotions flooded Anu as he stared upon his daughter and grandson. Thunderous turmoil raged behind his eyes as he stared her down, both pleased at her return and wounded from what she brought along with her. Fearing exile for her and her young child, Ninsun begged her father to let Gilmos stay in Eden. He did not belong to the realms of men, rather he belonged here where it was safe. Despite the love he felt for his daughter, and the spark of love he already felt forming within his chest for his own grandson; he had to refuse. Through tears of pain and fear, Ninsun cried out to her father to please; do as a king must and accept this powerless child into his kingdom. However, such a thing was not possible. The law was clear, the law that he wrote as king. To question his own word was to invite doubt and weakness into the minds of not only those who followed him, but potentially even himself.

"Ninsun, you know that none who bear the blood of man may reside here. Unless we wish for their sin and mortality to taint this world, we cannot allow a single one." Anu paused for a moment to look down upon his grandson.

"No matter how innocent they are." Ninsun fought back her tears, her hands quivering with desperation and rage.

"Nevertheless…" The king began, his own hand coming up to rub thoughtfully along his stubbled chin and cheeks. He thought of his wife, and how she might never forgive him if he turned away an infant child of their own cloth. How she would curse his name if he dared send this boy out into the world without a glimmer of protection.

"This is what I can do. I can grant my mortal grandson greater strength than that of a normal man. I will also grant him a much longer life, although he too shall return to the dirt one day. It would be wrong of me to favor one half-breed over another, even if he is of my blood. That is the only mercy I can give him." Anu murmured with a rather dejected tone. He cast his eyes towards the ground. While his word was law, that did not mean he did not feel a shred of shame from turning away his own flesh and blood.

"Father, how dare you! You let the fey have favor over your own grandson!" She paused for a moment to take a breath and steady herself. "I do recall what the first of humankind did to the tree. The world was young, and it was asked they not partake of it. Eating of the tree would grant them wisdom of all things good and evil, and they would cease to be the creatures you first made. They would be beasts filled with sin. But! My son is innocent! He should not suffer the sins of other men or that of his forefathers!" Ninsun said with a tear in her eye. Her teeth unconsciously bit into her lower lip as she tried her best to quell the pain within her heart. The Goddess stepped back as a wave of uncertainty, anger, envy, or jealousy fought to overtake her. She tightened her arms around the infant she held him, her eyes drifting towards the floor as she tried to come up with anything that could help her case.

"Nonetheless, he still carries that sin." Anu exhaled slowly as he slowly ran his hand down the side of his face. She glanced from her to the infant, and he could do nothing to stop his brow from furrowing with confusion and mild disdain.

"Now tell me, daughter, did this mortal at least hold value - or was he but a commoner?" While the question had a drop of venom into it, he placed a hand upon the back of her head in a rather fatherly fashion. He gently stroked her black hair with hope for a different outcome than the one burning in the center of his mind.

Ninsun looked at her father with an expression that was mildly calmer than before, her frown fading.

"It was a King.... King Lugalbanda." She paused for a moment and felt her jaw tighten. "But, what does it matter what the mortal's level is!?" The disgust towards her father was palpable. Why would he ask her such a question?

"Because, my dear, I can make a deal with one of the other deities. You are not the only goddess to fall for the beauty and seduction of man. But, it is shameful to talk about such things here and now." He placed his hand upon his chin while he tried to contemplate the situation. He let out a deep sigh before turning away to sit upon his throne. He sat there for several seconds before simply burying his face into his hands. His own stress at the situation was completely overwhelming him, and at this point he wanted to simply have a glass of ambrosia and go to sleep.

"I will speak with Enlil. Should Gilmos decide to wed his daughter Inu, his godhood shall be restored. Two demi-Gods can make a full-blooded god, if given divine blessing and sanction. Beyond that, there is a price you must pay." His voice lingered for a brief while as he found his daughter's gaze once more. His expression was stern and steady, and he patiently waited for his daughter to offer a response. She did nothing except wait and stare, her own face hardening with seriousness at the situation.

"Name it. I will do whatever it takes to protect my child." she said with a tone of strength and defiance. Even if she had to defy her father, he who had brought the very creation of the world and cosmos upon them all. For the child she clasped within her arms, she would do so for as long as it took.

"You must give up your immortality, my dear daughter." Anu muttered with a cold and patient tone. Ninsun opened her mouth in protest, but was swiftly silenced by a raised palm from her father.

"This is not up for discussion. I cannot allow such transgressions to pass without consequence, and let those who do so to traverse my land with impunity. Even you, my daughter. Furthermore, there is a possibility your son will refuse this offer. Men often prefer their free will, as I'm sure you well know." Tears once again found their way to her eyes, but she forced her expression to harden once again as she held her father's gaze. She would not back down, even if it meant her death. Which, in this case, it truly did. "If you make this choice, there is no going back. At one point or another, regardless of the outcome, I will send someone to earth to watch over your son and be his friend." Anu explained, hoping to soften his decree with some final embellishment that could put his daughter's mind to rest about the safety and well-being of her son. Urus stood silently nearby. Her presence hidden by stone pillars. Her mouth was thin as he wrapped his arms around her torso, although she did not dare speak on the events that transpired before her. She knew that even she was powerless to stop her husband once he had made up his mind about something. With a sorrowful step she turned and headed back towards her chambers. Her heart was heavy and her mind was clouded, but there was nothing she could do. While she did understand in some way, sending her grandson away and cursing their daughter to literal death was not something she could fully get behind. However, her acceptance on this matter was completely irrelevant. She would miss her daughter terribly, and being unable to meet and help raise her grandson would weigh on her terribly. Still, she had Arwen; and that was a comfort all on its own. Hopefully Anu would not take her away as well. With a disgusted and disappointed expression, Ninsun turned from her father and walked out of the throne room with her child still in her arms. She would do what any mother must. Her child was more important than anything. Her immortality, her place in the garden, even any feelings of loss or love she might have over anyone here. Things were different now, and the only thing that she could do was accept them. In fact, it was the only thing she could do for both of them for a mother will do whatever is in her power to protect her young.

Chapter 3:

Gilmos was brought back just like Anu had made Ninsun do. It was difficult for her as a mortal. Sadly, her time ruling with the King took a lousy turn. King Lugalbanda was very happy; his son would be among men. King Lugalbanda, however, would treat Ninsun very differently once she was stripped of her Goddess status. He did make her his queen since she bore him a son. King Lugalbanda laughed at Ninsun.

"So, your dead-beat father did not save you. You gave it all for him, but I thank you, for my healthy child. In the future maybe you can give me a second one someday." King Lugalbanda finally treated Ninsun like the woman she deserved to be upon the second year when she was with the child again. Gilmos seemed happy he was going to have a sibling. Gilmos would play with his little brother a lot and teach him all he knew. The two-year-old was filled with glow and light. When he was three and his little brother could walk, they play in the courtyard with the dogs and kick balls back and forth. The two small children would wrestle each other though. Gilmos mother would yell at him to take it easy on his little brother and she would make dry fruit for them as a treat. Then in the fourth year, a sad night happens filled with rain. The small two-year-old was left in a blanket alone and suffocated to death. Gilmos did not understand his brother's death, and it confused him sincerely where had his playmate left. Then King Lugalbanda would die in the war sometime after Gilmos's fourth birthday. Ninsun believed that King Lugalbanda did not die from wounds sustained in the war itself but from his sorrow of losing one son and how the wine-filled him to act as cruel as the first year of their marriage. Finally, when Gilmos started his private education at five. He made friends with two servant children Lee and Tamako. Lee was a half-fey child; both children also did not age fast, so it worked for them. When he was seven, he had a small crush on Lee. His crush did not last long, though. The reason was Gilmos, at the age of nine, was bitten whilst trying to protect her from a giant tiger. He then tried to kiss Lee, but she refused, which upset Gilmos as he felt he deserved it for trying to be a hero even if he failed.

This made him quickly get over his first love and possibly later fueled how he treated women. When he was ten, Ninsun would die from an illness that caused one to bring up blood from the eyes and mouth. Gilmos prayed every day to Anu. It seemed that Gilmos's prayers fell on deaf ears. Gilmos had heard the life stories of how things were in Eden. In the end, he had grown to hate the Gods because he felt they did not do enough for man and he blamed them for his mother's death. It was soon after his mother's death, he would dream of her and remember the promise of becoming a God. He did not want it, in any case. His anger was likely not only due to so many of his family being dead but also because of how he felt entitled and above others at times. While the young prince was growing up, Tamoko was kind enough to allow Gilmos around his family despite being a servant to Gilmos. Tamoko's family gave Gilmos a semi-ordinary life, but by the age of twelve, their prayers to the Gods and ritual practices made him upset that caused those wounds in him to fester and burn that the Gods did not answer him. When he was thirteen, he decided to run the palace like the young King he was, Of course, he had advisors since he was still a child. The prince had far more power than any other thirteen-year-old. Then finally, on his eighteenth birthday, he was crowned King of Babylon.

Chapter 4:

The enchantress as a child had no easy life. The enchantress's mother died in childbirth and that did not leave her much room to learn compassion or love. Inu was raised Amazons and Valkyries which caused her to feel as though she was stronger and less weak than others. The amazons worshipped her father's sister Ishtar who was not on the council of gods. This did however leave her room to see her father throughout her life. The sad truth of part of her mental issues was unfortunately her father's gifts were gifts of blood. If the small child did not get her way her father would kill the offender. Inu was spoiled rotten to the core. When Inu was just five she started to show some powers thought to be due to her goddess blood or maybe like her dear aunt a natural Mage. When Inu was ten she managed to help the Amazons and Valkyries take a lot of territory. Inu however did not agree with the idea of an only woman world. She battled the leader at thirteen and had her first victory. She caused the Valkyries and Amazons to split in their ideas. Some decided to follow her while others remained with their newfound faction. When she was sixteen, she gained even more ground and her father stepped in to teach her the dark arts. If there was any good left in Inu it was destroyed the day she ripped out the heart of a unicorn that was left by her dead mother. It was a test both Ishtar and her father gave her. Then by twenty-one, she was ready to meet the slightly younger prince who was now king. Anu and Enlil came to Gilmos.

"My dear grandson, I had come for the promise that was made when you were an infant. I present to you Enlil; he shall bring you to his daughter," Anu said as he brought his hand out to introduce Enlil.

"You come into *my* Kingdom when *you* let my mother, and my father dies, never lifting a finger to help...... I spit on your name! Do not dare speak that you were my grandfather when you did not answer a single prayer!" Gilmos spoke to Anu with no respect.

Luckily, Anu was a kind God and had already brought Inu without even asking and would have Enlil introduce his daughter either way.

"Your highness, forgive your grandfather's laziness and allow me to introduce to you Inu, the enchantress," Enlil said as some of the fey brought in a woman who wore a red silk dress with a black veil upon her face, and she had blood-red hair, and dark yellow eyes, to Gilmos she looked like some kind of demonic bride

"King Gilmos, I have commanded many and taken over many lands with my magic, so I believe I am fit to be your queen, and as an added gift, you will be granted the status of a God as well, does this not please you, my lord?" she asked. As she removed the veil from her face, Gilmos noticed that she was holding a bouquet in her hands. Gilmos tried not to laugh, but he could not help himself.

"As I told these two Gods, I am not interested. I will find glory on my own, not by your hands, or theirs! You are nothing to me! You Gods only care that there is a statue or you here and there. I have heard the stories of you Inu, you kill your soldiers for sport!" Gilmos said. Inu began to get upset at Gilmos' words.

"You refuse me when you are no better and are a tyrant, I give you this last chance to accept their offer, or you will regret the day you met me.," she said as she snapped her fingers, disappearing in a flash as the flowers fall to the floor.

"To kill for loyalty and to kill for sport are different. A queen must be her King's match and equal. You, on the other hand, are nothing but the Gods' little pet, and only agree for your lust for power," Gilmos said. Anu and Enlil left though they tried their best to change Gilmos mind because they knew very well that this would cause a split between the Gods. Inu had already begun plotting her harsh haunting revenge. She would not forget the rejection and embarrassment the King caused her that day. It had put a dent in her pride and her perfect record of getting what she wanted.

Chapter 5:

There is rarely such a thing that blinds as effectively as one's own hubris. This was a lesson that King Gilmos had yet to learn, nor would he likely remember lest it was not learnt in blood. Like a prowling panther hidden just beyond the warm glow of the campfire, the reckoning that sought to swallow Gilmos' whole was crouched just out of reach and out of sight. The young man was completely oblivious to the fact that The Enchantress had called upon the demons from the underworld to aid her repayment of the disrespect that was so callously placed at her feet. Her connections to the underworld and those that dwelled within it were easy enough to come by, giving her mystical and divine heritage. All she needed to do was ferry a few souls to the Underworld, and agree to lend her aid in a few key wars and battles to come; she could have everything she needed to deliver what she promised upon the arrogant king. With her silent rage and growing discontent, so too did the lands surrounding Gilmos' abode begin to darken and decay. The skies were stricken with a palpable uneasiness that one could practically taste. Unfortunately, ignorance is bliss; at least, until the illusion is broken. When Arwen came of age, she was sent to the land of man as promised many, many moons ago. Urus and Anu were quite sad to see their beloved pseudo-child depart, but they tried to take solace in the gorgeous smile that was plastered upon Arwen's face when she was told where she was going. With a leap of joy. She launched herself into their arms. She nearly knocked them over as her arms coiled around their shoulders as tightly as possible. The young fey thanked them over and over again as she practically vibrated with excitement. Her bright eyes practically glowing as tears of joy threatened to flow down her cheeks. Without even gathering any of her belongings, she practically skipped off towards the edge of their reality, not wishing to spend any more time than she absolutely had to outside of the land of man. Arwen traveled through the woods for many moons. Her progress towards King Gilmos should have taken a fortnight at the very latest. However, the young maiden kept getting distracted by all the sorts of wildlife that roamed the surrounding forests. She even picked some flowers and made them into a small crown for herself, although she could already tell that the life here was not quite cut from the same cloth as back home. Before too long, she traversed the forest and mountains beyond. Upon reaching the summit, she peered out across the vast landscape. Her white dress flowed around her in the wind, which made her appear almost like an angelic presence. Her eyes rested upon the Kingdom of legends as it lay still in the sand. The scent of flowers and fresh food wafted out from within the walls, tempting all passersby to enter and share their wares and wealth. Even from here she could see the walls were laced with gold and silver. No doubt a rarity for the time and place. There were many guards along the palace walls. The guards each adorned with shields and light armor. Which was a necessity in the desert heat. Arwen decided that she would look for a way into the castle from the back. After much searching, she finally found a path where the water leads into the Kingdom. Following the flow of water upstream, she swam underneath the gate and slipped beneath the wall of the kingdom without being noticed. With an almost playful giggle, she began nimbly ducking and dancing through the streets and alleys. It was practically a game at this point, and the end goal was to get to the castle without being seen or stopped. Before noon she found her way to the castle in the center of the city, and scaling the wall into one of the lower windows was easy enough for someone with her level of dexterity. She searched each room very carefully, although each door yielded nothing of interest as she came closer and closer to the throne room. As she pressed her ear to the door of the throne room, she felt a hand clasp upon her wrist. Her grip tightened on the doorknob as she whirled around to face the person who had found her, and she practically burst out laughing at the ridiculous hat upon the man's head.

"No one is allowed within this chamber! How did a mere peasant girl make her way this far?!" the jester asked with a rough jerk of his hand. He twisted his body to try and wrench Arwen's wrist around, clearly intent on putting her in some kind of hold. His face was filled with bewilderment when the girl hardly moved, in fact she was hardly budged an inch except for the constant giggling coming from her ruby lips.

"Please unhand me, sir. I am no mere commoner. Rather, I have been sent here on behalf of King Anu and Queen Urus!" she explained as she gently pulled her wrist away from the servant man. Despite the clear struggle from the jester, he watched as her wrist slipped freely from his grasp with very little effort on her part. Before he could resume chastising the strange woman, the King had turned into the hall and began making his way towards the pair. His steps slowed as he moved closer and closer, his brow furrowed as he studied the woman's immaculate beauty. A deep purr rumbled in his throat as his eyes scanned her up and down, and his smile and expression were unmistakable as he ran his hand through his thick locks.

"Well, what do we have here? Someone from the city that wishes to offer herself as my queen?" Gizmos could hardly stifle his laugh as he looked upon his servant. His tone and constant glances towards Arwen indicated that was not entirely joking.

Tamoko before he could even respond, Arwen spoke up whilst completely turning her body towards the young king. "Forgive me, but I am no mere plaything. Anu, your grandfather, has sent me to warn you of Inu's vengeful plans. The plans to bring ruin upon you and your kingdom to ruin." Her tone was stern but patient, a testament to the nature of the woman who raised her. Gilmos had to admit that she spoke and acted with a similar strength to his mother, although for what reason this could possibly be; he had no idea. Gilmos casually dismissed the jester with a wave of his hand, his eyes still fully locked on the beautiful woman who was still intruding within his home.

"I hope the trip was worth it. I have no need for you or whatever information you might bring. I am already aware that the enchantress is likely planning something, and whatever it is I am certain me and my men will be able to handle it."

Gilmos sighed softly as he shamelessly cast his eyes up and down the young maiden once more.

"If you wish to stay to warm my bed instead, you may. But for the battle itself, I have no use for the efforts of a girl hardly bigger than a lion's cub." Gilmos said in a dismissively arrogant tone.

"I can beat you in a sword fight, for I am no cub but have the mighty strength of a full-grown lioness " she inquired, her knowing smile exposing a set of immaculate white teeth. After a brief pause to look around the room, she nodded towards a rack of weapons that stood against the far wall. "Grab me one, if you don't mind. You may grab one for yourself as well. If you win, I'll let you take me to your chambers. *When* I win, you wipe that disgusting smirk off your lips and actually listen for once in your life. How's that?" As if her tone and sass wasn't enough to capture his attention, the thought of getting to bed this woman for simply beating her in a duel was too good to pass up. The King practically sprinted over to the rack and retrieved two one-handed swords. With a haphazard and intentionally poor throw, he chucked the sword towards the girl blade first.

"As you wish." he muttered with a strange blend of intrigue and disinterest. He was clearly curious about what made her so confident, but he was also so sure of himself that he was certain that the fight didn't demand his full attention.

"First to draw blood wins. I'll try to keep my strikes below the shoulder. I would hate to scar that pretty little face of yours." Gilmos said with a dismissive scoff. His eyes widened as he watched the young girl in the white dress casually twirl and swing the blade effortlessly in one hand. With a patient stare she raised her blade to him, silently inviting him to come forth and take the first swing.

With a quick nod, Gilmos rushed forward and swung the blade in a very telegraphed arc with his right hand. The intention was to wait for Arwen to predictably block or take a strike at his open stomach, in which he would turn his body and parry the blade; then score a hit upon her wrist or forearm. However, Arwen was not only faster and stronger; but she was far more versatile with a blade than he could ever hope to be. The training he received while growing up was poultry compared to what she'd done throughout her many years in The Garden. Arwen seemingly fell for the bait, taking a flat and wide swing at Gilmos' open stomach as he swung in. Once the king attempted to turn his body and parry the incoming blade, Arwen turned her own body to catch the blade as it came in. With the king's blade pinned between his own body and Arwen's blade, he was powerless to stop or avoid the punch that came for the left side of his face. He cried out in pain as her fist smashed into his jaw, sending him flying back a few feet and landing on his ass. As he fell backwards, Arwen swiped her sword with an upward stroke and casually nicked his forearm. Gilmos laid there for a moment, his sword having spun away across the floor. He held his arm up to inspect the blood flowing freely from it, and he continuously opened and closed his mouth to try and help the pain flee his jaw. The young maiden slowly walked forward and casually kicked the sword further away, sending it spinning back towards the rack on the opposite side of the room. With a flick of her wrist, she tossed the blade back towards the rack; and it expertly fell back within its holder with a loud thud.

"I believe that's checkmate, the queen takes the knight, or the queen takes the King. By the way, this girl has a name, and my name is Arwen. When you're done being a pig of a man, and you decide you're ready to accept my help to save you and your kingdom; come find me." she said and with that, Arwen turned on her heels and exited the throne room; leaving the King to lay there stunned, wounded in pride and body, and drawn to her like a butterfly to a flower.

Chapter 6:

Upon being granted quarters to reside in during her time in the castle. Arwen quickly excused herself and retreated to the room to think. She no longer felt confident regarding her mission. While it was early, the king just seemed far too full of himself to even dream of taking on Inu and her vast wealth of knowledge and power. It boggled her mind to even contemplate how someone so cocky could even be related to Anu. While every God had a certain measure of pride about themselves and the realm, they held dominion over. This seemed to be another matter entirely; and the king didn't even have any powers to speak. At least, none that she could see. Beyond mere appearance, Arwen couldn't find any real common ground between Gilmos and Arwen, even taking into account the generational gap between them. With a deep sigh, she laid back on the silky linens of her Cerulean-drowned bed. She threw herself into the cotton ball-like pillows and let out an exasperated sigh. After a moment of contemplation, she slid down from the bed and knelt onto the floor. A small, clear, crystal quartz dangled from around her neck. With a quick flick of her fingers, she swung it left and right like a pendulum, her gorgeous eyes focusing heavily on it as it swung back and forth. After a while the necklace began to glow, and from within an image took form in the air.

"Yes, my sweet? Is something the matter? I didn't expect you to report back so quickly." Queen Urus murmured, a tone and expression of worry already etched into her features and speech.

"My Queen, how do you expect me to help this arrogant brat? He speaks so awfully of you, and hardly even recognizes any ability I might have! I have never met someone so insolent in my life!" she explained, her own frustration and exasperation at the situation clearly showing.

With a wry smile, Queen Urus offered a small sigh and a nod of understanding.

"Patience, my love. He has had quite the hard life. Remember, mortals see death, pain, and hardship far beyond what we do; especially within The Garden. Do not be so hard on him, at least until you sit down with him and try to understand how he became the way he is."

"Would you, or the King, be mad at me if I left this dreadful place? I... I want to explore the world of men and see what it has to offer. See those beautiful mountains I've heard so much about, and taste the delicious foods from the other side of the world. There's so much here to experience, I don't want to waste my time with this…" she paused for a moment and let out a quiet huff.

"This idiot.." Queen Urus brought her hand up to cover her mouth, but Arwen could tell that Urus was just trying to hide the giggle that tried to spill from her lips. With a warm but slightly pained smile, Arwen continued.

"You know that I am loyal, and I will always do whatever you ask of me. It's just...so difficult being around such a selfish and disgusting person. I'm surprised he hasn't tried to lay a hand on my rear yet!" Arwen said with yet another exasperated groan. She reached up for the blanket and pulled it over her head and shoulders like a shawl, her expression of discontent clear as day.

"My love, you know that we will not force you to stay there if you don't want to. Nor will we punish you for how you feel or what you wish to do. While you are there on our behest, you still have your own free will. You are not our slave; you are our darling angel; and we will support you always." Urus murmured with a loving, motherly tone. After a slow exhalation through her nose, Arwen gave an understanding nod and stared longingly into her queen's eyes.

"I'll think about it...But...I miss you..." she muttered softly. Despite her excitement at coming here, it was undeniable that she missed being home. She missed being able to wrap her arms around her queen and king, as well as her kin. The sentimental moment was quickly shattered as Arwen's head snapped up towards the door to her room. Hearing footsteps begin shuffling away from her room, she quickly flicked her thumb against the necklace and spun it around its holder. As she ascended and made her way towards the door, she refastened the necklace around her neck and tucked it under her shirt. After throwing the door open, Arwen would see that ridiculous looking jester skulking away. He was now a mere ten feet from the door to her room. The sheepish expression on the lad's face told her all she needed to know.

"I don't know about you, but where I come from; eavesdropping is considered incredibly rude." Arwen growled, her eyes staring with even more annoyance than before. Was everyone in this god forsaken castle just completely devoid of manners or courtesy?

"You would leave us after you fought so hard to prove a point?" asked Tamako, completely ignoring Arwen's initial question.

"What does it matter to you, trickster?" Arwen huffed, clearly not interested in discussing her plans or desires in this regard.

"What if I could show you that the King has a different side? That he is not simply a man who cares for no one but himself?" Tamako offered, his lips pursing together as if to say

'Ehh?' "Maybe, just maybe, if you look past his bitterness, you may find a certain...sweetness?" Never wasting a moment to make a joke, Tamako began expertly tossing lemons in the air.

"You say he isn't as bad as he seems, and yet he orders you around and even belittles you in fashion choice?" Arwen muttered, gesturing towards his ridiculous outfit and hat. Then a lingering silence between them, she sighed and carefully rubbed her face.

"Very well. I will give you one week to show me that the King is not as bad as he seems." she muttered with a quick roll of her eyes. With that she turned back towards her room. Upon crossing the threshold, she turned her head and poked her head back out into the hallway.

"Also, next time I catch you spying on me; I'll ring your head like a bell, much like a bat with rabies." With that, she slammed the door shut and retired to her bed to rest.

Chapter 7:

In the coming weeks, she ended up watching The King at the oddest moments. To say she had mixed feelings would be quite the understatement; however, she decided to give the advice of the dorky jester a try. It wasn't as if she had anything to really lose, except her preconceived notions of the man. The king was very good to his dogs and one would without fully understanding the other might believe he kept them around simply for protection. Arwen however looked deeper into why they also have large beasts if the dogs were merely tools to the king. In the group of dogs, there were five puppies. There were two the king seemed to handle more. The first was a very energetic blonde one who did not mind her business. The king seemed to enjoy her energy. The second one born seemed to be the smallest one. The puppy was quite unique compared to the rest with her black and brown fur, and its exceptional fluff. One evening, one of the other pups had been a bit too rough with its play; and accidently landed wrong on the youngling. Amidst the screeching and hollering, it was discovered that the puppy's legs had been broken. With a semblance of panic in his mannerisms, the King personally escorted the crying animal to the stables where it would be helped and mended as quickly as possible. Upon being returned to the litter, the pup snuggled up affectionately to its mother while she licked and sniffed them to check if they were alright.

"Does the king…show compassion? I thought only Anu showed mercy to living things. We are taught mankind has no mercy, yet he cares for this little fluffy dog. He cares for them like the Gods of Life care for their own. It's so…strange." she said to Tamako. Though tears were rarely, if ever, shed; his demeanor and expressions told much of his inner turmoil. The King was never much for outward expressions of emotion, except evidently rage and wrath. Still, his silence spoke volumes. One day, Gilmos noticed her gawking as he tended to another one of the pups.

"Don't just stand there. Either make yourself useful or leave my presence!" he snapped at her, although for once his tone lacked the typical cruelty that often laced his words.

With an almost amused smile, Arwin pushed herself off the wall and took a few patient steps towards him. In his hands lay another golden pup, and while it seemed to be quite happy; his fingers prying at her mouth seemed to indicate something was wrong. "Mmm? What problem can the great king not solve for his dogs?" she asked in an almost mocking tone. As she looked at him, she pushed her purple hair back over her shoulder.

"Surely the fey take care of the animals of the garden, do they not? If so, tell me; what do you do for a dog with little weight and gums that look like this." He asked her, gesturing down to the mildly struggling pup in his grasp. Its teeth appeared to be mostly fine, however around the gums of one of its teeth; there appeared to be significant inflammation. As Arwin's eyes explored the dog, it did appear to be a bit thinner than what was probably healthy for its age.

Arwin sat down and held the young pup who seemed to take a liking to her very quickly. She looked at the young female dog's blistered gums. With a small sound of pity, she felt the poor pup's bones that were visibly through her skin. Given that she had seen the king and watched his manner of care for the animal, it was safe to presume that he had not abused the dog. After releasing the dog, she quietly tapped her foot on the floor and began to think of things that could help the small animal feel better.

"First, I am going to need a bowl and the plant "Aloe Vera". I trust you have some apothecary that could fetch that if you do not already have it on hand. They need to smash it into a gel, then smear it onto her gums a couple times a day. Over time, that should ease her gums and reduce the pain." Arwin said. Without a moment's hesitation, Gilmos snapped his fingers at the servants that stood close by. They bowed their heads and offered a small nod, already able to figure out their orders without requiring direct instruction.

"As for her weight, you can add eggs to her diet. Chicken would not be a bad idea, but make sure the bones are removed or she could choke on them. Also, you can add fish and smashed pumpkin to her diet. All these things are fairly high in calories and are a good start to helping her gain more weight." Arwin said in a cheerful but matter-of-fact tone.

The King pulled out a piece of parchment and scrawled the ingredients onto it before handing it to a nearby servant. "Thank you," Gilmos murmured quietly, his eyes still focused on the creature as it waddled back towards its siblings.

"You're welcome." She paused for a moment before adding "Just so we're clear, I am doing this for them, not you." she said to him.

Gilmos furrowed his brow slightly as Arwin turned to leave, and stayed silent as he watched her depart. Once Tamako came by and peered into the enclosure with the pups, Gilmos gave a slight turn while keeping his eyes on the doorway.

"Her tongue is quite sharp, is it not?" Gilmos said to his friend.

"It would seem so. Give her some time to warm up to you, and maybe hold back on your insults. If you don't, you might very well push her away from you," Tamoko said to him.

"Let's not get any crazy ideas, Tamoko. I am being cordial to the girl, and I am simply commenting on an aspect of her personality that I seem to admire. Do not start with any nuptial agreements yet." he murmured dismissively before departing to handle other matters.

Chapter 8:

A few days passed and Arwen noticed the king was nowhere in the palace. Arwen decided if the king was going, she would explore the town. Arwen noticed that there were many people in the kingdom. She noticed that some were well off while others were not lucky enough to have shoes. Arwen heard a little girl crying in the street. The poor little girl was thin to the bone. She then gave the small child an apple that she had in her light purple lavender bag. After the girl profusely thanked her. Arwen gave her a small pat on the head and continued on her way. As she continued her journey, she felt a deep pain in her heart for the people. Part of her wanted to be angry at the king. How could he abandon his people in such a way?

Then much to her surprise she watched the King disguise himself as a homeless man and take with him a basket full of bread which he took the time to give to the homeless. She was shocked that a man who wore so much gold and the finest clothes in Babylon would hide his identity from his people. As she saw him give the bread to the people her fury slowly disappeared. While she was filled with bewilderment, she could see he cared for his people. "Why would a ruler hide that they were trying to help those who had less?" she thought to herself. With a confident stride, Arwen began to approach him to confront his methods and intentions. Surely there was a much more effective method of doing this and one that made a difference for the people. After taking no less than two steps; Arwen felt a firm hand rest on her shoulder.

"The king won't be happy if he finds out you did not stay where he asked..." Tamako mused. Arwen narrowed her eyes at the jester she could tell that he was sincerely warning her. She knew that the king did not like those who tested him or did not do as they were told, although that wasn't her concern.

"I can go where I like, you and Gilmos are not in charge of me," she exclaimed with a deep venom to her tone. She had been controlled by the gods for most of her life, she would certainly not let any human do the same thing. Despite the glare from her eyes, she let out a sigh and decided that she was not going to get to speak with the king at this moment. She would, however, ask the question that was burning in her mind. She watched the annoying jester for a brief moment before opening her mouth to speak.

"Why does the King not tell the people who he is?" she asked Tamako. Her expression was filled with confusion and disbelief, similar to how a child might look upon someone. She knew that the jester was far more knowledgeable of this man and character, and despite her reservations against the man; his expertise was worth a fair bit, at least in this circumstance. Furthermore, hiding one's deeds and desires wasn't something she was familiar with. As far as she knew, everyone in the Garden was upfront about their desires and plans.

"He was taught from a young age that one must never boast about performing a noble task. A good deed must be done because it is the right thing to do, not because one seeks a reward." Tamako said to the girl. "He could certainly use his magnanimous nature and use it to bolster his reign and gain popularity, but that simply isn't his way. He does not concern himself with the opinions of other people, negative or positive. He simply does what he thinks is best, and whatever comes from it is out of his control."

Chapter 9:

Some time passed and she saw the King cooking with no help from the staff. This confused Arwen quite a bit, especially considering, in Eden, the Gods never cooked for themselves. She had heard stories about royal figures on the human plane; and how they explicitly had servants handle such things. That kind of work was beneath them, in a manner of speaking. One could say that she was rather spoiled; even though she didn't particularly hold herself with nearly as much pomposity as the King did. Arwen decided that this was something she wanted to learn despite her lack of experience in mind. The fact that he could cook, seemingly without the assistance of others or reading materials, was rather attractive. It went without saying that she would never admit such things out loud, and she even went as far as mentally chastising herself for even having such a thought.

With a slightly flustered expression, she approached the jester; who, as usual, stood near the king. Thankfully her poker face was on by the time he lifted his head to address her.

"Your King…. cooks? I…I don't quite understand. He's noble, and a male at that. I can't even cook! If I did, I fear I burn the food till it was black like charcoal." Arwen said with a slight whine of disbelief.

After studying the young woman for a moment, he smirked briefly and lightly prodded her nose.

"You're red like a tomato! Is it too hot in here, or did you accidentally burn your cheeks over his fire?" Tamako said joking with the fairy.

"My face is not red! It's just…slightly pink like a…like a lotus sitting steadily on the water." Arwen declared, her eyes glaring daggers at the man. Even so, she unintentionally sounded quite pouty.

"I'm simply poking a bit of fun," he assured her. He briefly motioned down to his attire. "It is quite literally my job. I'm sure the little fairy can take a joke, no?" He gave a cheeky grin before continuing. "In any case, The King has many skills, since he has had to raise himself and all. Despite having many subjects at his hand and foot, certain…events have hardened him and encouraged him to keep us at arm's length."

She mused for a brief moment, her eyes staring beyond the doorway to observe the man continuing to put spices and garnish into whatever he was making.

"But, then I forget how damaged you fey are-" he continued. "So clueless except for the task you are given." Upon casting a knowing glance to the side, he continued with his teasing; but this time seemingly with a purpose. "But, I suppose, since you asked so nicely; I can show you a trick or two. You seem like you want to impress him."

"I didn't even-" Arwen began.

"Come along! I don't have all day." Tamako exclaimed. Then, just as the king exited the kitchen with his bowl and goblet in hand; Tamako guided Arwen in and threw an apron at her face. Some cooking lessons would do her well, regardless if she was trying to impress his lord or not.

Chapter 10:

Unbeknownst to her, while Arwen was spying on the King during the day, the king was returning the favor during the evening. It was only fair that he study her while she did the same for him. There was one night in particular when she caught his eye. Gilmos heard a soft voice in the hallway outside of his room. He scoured the halls for what felt like hours, chasing its echo until he could identify its source. He finally was able to locate it wafting through the doorway to one of the many studies within his castle. With a slightly furrowed brow, he entered and continued making his way onward. Much to his surprise, he saw Arwen singing to a little red fox that she had managed to slip into the palace. Whether she brought it from home or purchased it from some merchant, he did not know. She seemed quite fond of it. Perhaps it reminded her of something. Arwen continued with her pleasant melody, and she cheerfully walked the little fox to the balcony. She lifted her gaze up towards the stars and sighed softly as the sound of the surrounding wildlife seemed to blend with her song.

"So, she likes foxes too…" Gizmos silently mused. "The birds seem to enjoy her melody as well." he thought. His thoughts drifted back to his room; his mind's eye settling on the owl, fox, bear, and wolf statues there.

His chambers and hallways were full of sculptures of the wild life. She seemed to care for the fox as much as he cared for the puppy, and he suspected that care might extend to all living creatures. After all, he could recall how she helped with the dogs whenever she was able to. He was rather charmed that she was good with animals.

"Good with a sword, kind and welcoming with the animals. Maybe the fey is not so different from us. She's a bit headstrong but…she's sweet." he thought to himself as he walked away. He silently skulked out of the study, taking great care to ensure that he was not found during his escape.

Chapter 11:

On the second month on a cold night, Arwen helped a small child whom she had never seen before. It puzzled her greatly to see a young child scampering through the halls without anyone watching him. But, then again, it wouldn't be the first thing that had confused her since arriving here. The young boy had fallen and was quietly crying near a large pillar whilst rubbing his knee. With a small frown of concern, Arwen approached the boy and knelt beside him.

"Are you hurt? Here, let me help you up. Let's go find your parents." She spoke. The boy sniffed and nodded before taking the woman's hand. She gently pulled him up to his feet and brushed her hand across his clothes to dust him off.

"You know, I get lost in this big old castle too," she said with a soft smile.

The young boy looked at her for several seconds, seemingly studying her with great wonder and curiosity.

"You're a fairy, right? Grandmother told me all about the fairy people and their wings." Arwen offered a small smile as the boy continued.

"My grandma works in the third-highest tower of the King's castle! She makes all the best clothes in Babylon." said the little child.

"Then that is where we will go." She grabbed the boy's hand and began pulling him down to the hall in a gentle manner. "And we do, but the wings are not always visible; we typically only call on them when we are happy," Arwen said with a soft smile

"Are you not happy then, fairy lady?" the child asked. She paused for a moment before deciding how to respond.

"I am confused by your King. Not that it's anything you have to worry about," she said smiling. It was clear even to him that she was attempting to brush the words off.

"Okay… if you say so fairy lady. My grandma says people should speak their minds. Even the king just has a hard time showing his feelings. She says it's because some men learn not to show that they are sensitive, but I think that's silly. Girls should be strong and boys should be allowed to cry." the child said.

"Your grandmother sounds like a wise woman." Arwen listened to the boy's regurgitation of his grandmother's words.

"I suppose it's true, some creatures do create ideas that are harmful to their own. It comes with setting up expectations." Arwen said as she picked up the child, intent on hurrying him along so she could get back to her other activities.

"What are expectations?" the small child asked, gently clinging to her shirt as she carried him.

"Oh, I am sorry. What I mean is when a person has a belief that something should be or turn out one way over another," she said in a very kind manner. The small child let out a sound of acknowledgment before nuzzling into her bosom. Arwen blushed ever so slightly but did not attempt to move the child from his resting position.

By the time they got to the third floor of the tower, the child had fully fallen asleep in her arms. Upon arriving in the tower, she silently handed the sleeping child to the mother. She gave a courteous nod to Gilmos who was sitting patiently within the tower, seemingly waiting for his newest sets of clothing to be brought to him. As Arwen left the tower, Gilmos found himself lost deep in thought.

"I don't get it, she seems to possess maternal instincts and yet does not seem to have children of her own. That is not even her seed!" he thought to himself. After some more contemplation, a soft smirk crossed his lips.

"No, no, you're not thinking a fey could be a mother. Especially with a human, of all things," he said to himself shaking his head. Despite his attempts to fight his inner thoughts, he found himself drawn to her like a moth to a flame. Upon her descent, Arwen slipped on the steps and ripped her dress. With a tired and annoyed sigh, Arwen trudged back up and went to speak with the seamstress. As a token of appreciation for returning her grandson, the grandmother offered to make Arwen a dress completely free of charge. However, with a gracious smile, Arwen shook her head and instead asked the seamstress to teach her how to fix the gown. During this entire exchange, Gilmos sat there silently with his hands folded in his lap.

"Why would a spoiled fey learn to sew? It was obvious the woman was grateful to her for returning her offspring to her, and yet she refused to accept the favor in return. Rather, she asked for nothing in return but knowledge?" Gilmos quietly tapped his fingers together while he studied Arwen, seemingly trying to figure out this enigmatic creature.

Chapter 12:

In the fourth month, Arwen brought the King breakfast. Her skills had improved quite a bit since her last attempt, although it wasn't as good as the king. The king eyed the food and gave a little chuckle before making a small joke.

"Finally, you show yourself. It would seem that Tamako has been showing you around the kitchen, as well as…other areas." He paused for a moment and lightly rubbed his face with his hand.

"It's flattering that you find me interesting enough to spy on me. Learn anything interesting, servant, of the deities?" he said in a somewhat pleasant tone. While there was a slight edge to his words, the playful manner and jester-like smirk implied that he was simply having a bit of fun. What caught her attention was that he seemed rather proud that he had figured out what she was doing. Under normal circumstances, she would have expected someone finding out they were being spied on to go much worse. Refocusing her attention on the topic at hand, Arwen crossed her arms and addressed the King with a playful jab of her own.

"Why do you not show everyone how kind you are? Would the people not love you more if you showed them this kindness over the harshness?" Arwen asked curiously.

The brief pause from Gilmos informed her of everything she needed to know. It appeared that he wasn't completely aware of the level of observation she had been doing, or for how long.

"Not bad" he began before taking a small sniff of his plate.

"For a novice, anyway. We'll make something together tomorrow, see if you can keep your composure while I'm around. And, to answer your question, a King should show strength and firmness far more often than not. Kindness can easily be perceived as weakness." He took a brief moment and held up his utensil, which showed a piece of decently-cooked meat.

"Sort of like cooking! It takes a firm hand mixed with a special sort of golden touch. You must trust yourself and your choices, and make sure not to add too much, or too little, of one thing. Otherwise, it throws the entire balance off, and the dish suffers." Gilmos said as he studied the meal Arwen had made with careful eyes.

"You don't trust me?!" she asked, almost demonstrably offended by the fact it had taken him this long to even take a bite of the food she prepared for him.

"I am the servant of the Gods, as you just said! Where we come from should not decide who we are! You, of all people, should understand that since you come from the Gods, even though you deny your divine blood!" Arwen exclaimed, her hands trembling with rage. Despite the king's mildly aloof nature, it was clear to him that she was upset that her dish wasn't even worthy of commentary or appreciation. Tears of frustration fell down her cheeks as she stood there trembling. She knew that her words did not make much sense, but it was difficult for her to express how her feelings of isolation and like she didn't belong were bubbling forth at this moment.

"You have a valid point, little one. Indeed, you might be smarter and wiser than I originally anticipated. That being said, your temper needs to cool. Rage and disgraceful behavior are unbecoming of you. Besides, life would be boring if there were no room for improvement, mm?" he murmured patiently. He reached up and lightly pinched her cheek with his thumb and forefinger, which no doubt caused her cheeks to flush slightly. Thankfully, they were already heated from her prior outburst, so it was difficult to tell.

"I'm sorry, I am not used to not being perfect." she mumbled with a certain air of embarrassment.

"You need not worry. Maybe you can teach me a thing or two tomorrow, hm? In any case, I appreciate the meal. Thank you very much." Gilmos said with a warm smile. With that, he gave a small wave of his hand and dismissed her.

Chapter 13:

Before the sun had barely crested over the horizon to announce the following day, Arwen decided to do some painting in the courtyard. She was doing her best to capture the majesty of the sunrise as it ascended over the mountains, as well as the lilies that swirled with the waters that fell off from a faraway city that was carved into the aforementioned mountains. The colors were not easy to capture in all their beauty, especially with how rich the purples, reds, and oranges were for the flowers. It was almost as if each of them wanted to be the center of attention for her painting, and she found herself smiling wryly as she worked. There was so much life to capture within her painting that she found herself having to exclude certain things just to keep her composition from getting crowded. She opted to simply paint a small family of frogs, along with a cute turtle with yellow and red on its cheeks. She heard the door to the terrace open, and she silently glanced to the side to see the king approach.

"You're up early?" he mused while stretching his arms above his head.

"That is when nature is most musical," she said, clearly speaking from a place of knowledge and experience. She turned to him for a brief moment to take in his form and attire before focusing once more on her artwork. After a moment of silence, Gilmos stepped forward and eyed her painting curiously.

"I have always been curious about art, but never found the time to learn. Perhaps you can assist me in learning?" he said to her.

"Well, I suppose that is only fair. You intend on teaching me to cook later today, so we should have time for a small lesson; right?" she said with a small tilt of her head. She briefly dunked her brushes into a few cups of water to rinse them off their paint. She then roughly smacked them against the legs of one of her easels to remove any excess water. As she did so, she briefly met the king's gaze and gestured for him to sit.

She picked up a light and transparent paper made from bamboo and gently affixed it to a makeshift frame that she created using some sticks she had found. Arwen was far too proud of her painting to break it down prematurely, so she opted to take the time to make the King his setup instead.

"Interesting. Your paper is not made of bones?" he asked with a curious tone. He gently ran his fingers along its smooth surface, almost as if this were his first-time seeing paper constructed from new material.

"I did some looking around, and I found this paper from a nearby city. The people there, much like you, show promise for humanity's advances. Though, what surprised me, was that unlike most humans they seem to show high respect for the creatures and the gods." she mused with a slight click of her tongue.

"I know the city of which you speak. They call my bitter grandfather "Shangdi" rather than "Anu", do they not?"

Gilmos murmured as he reached down to grasp one of the brushes.

"Indeed, it was a bit strange. Their customs and religious practices are similar to ours, but…just slightly different with their interpretations," she said. She was visibly confused and didn't quite know what to make of those people, but she seemed to harbor no ill will towards their differences.

"There are many other humans with many different languages. But, we are the oldest and first to speak; as far as anyone knows," he said, that familiar cockiness and pride emanating throughout his speech again. Before Arwen could turn to chastise him for his arrogance, she gave a small raise of her eyebrow at the piece he appeared to be working on. Even without prior instruction, Gilmos seemed to understand that painting was done in layers. The base of his creation had very similar colors and outlines to her own, although the colors were not as equally mixed nor the lines as well painted.

A strange flutter filled her chest. Now it was her turn to feel pride in the fact that Gilmos had opted to try and recreate what she made. Whether he was inspired by her painting, or it was the easiest thing to think of in the short time they were sitting together; she didn't care. It felt good to be acknowledged.

"In any case, Lord Gilmos; try and match what I do," she said with a small giggle. His wrist was excessively stiff for the type of shapes and movements that she was having him do, but it amused her quite a bit. It was like teaching a child to walk for the first time. Even with the light pumping of his ego with the word

"Lord", she could see the mounting annoyance and exasperation on his features as they worked together.

"It takes practice, as you say. It's all about shapes, at least in the beginning" she said with more and more giggles slipping out.

"It looks like a child's work!" he declared; a visible scowl etched into his features. He scoffed and wiped his hand onto his tunic, then looked down and cursed at his mistake; which resulted in him painting his attire with splotches of red and blue.

"Gah! Son of a" he said with a hint of frustration as he looked at his painting upset it did not turn out how he wished it to.

"If you won't finish yours, then I will give you mine when it's complete," she said, cutting him off from his expletives with an award-winning smile. The king turned to her and swiftly blew air through his pressed lips. Despite his slight pouting, he thanked her and turned to leave. Before he could even exit the terrace, Tamoko opened the door for him and began blustering about his kingly duties for the day.

Chapter 14:

The following morning arrived, and Gilmos met the girl in the kitchen and thought. The King watched Arwen mix eggs, then pulled her hand away and grabbed a second bowl and eggs.

"Not like that, like this - use a whisk. Never a spoon or a fork. Cooking is like painting; you must use the appropriate tools for the job," he said to her and mixed it, then allowed her to try the next one. Then they moved on to the bread that was to be placed in the fire stove.

"Never make it too dark or too light," he explained to her. Then they got onto the steak.

"This must be a dark brown. Too much blood is bad," he explained to her. Arwen was a little hesitant to cook meat, for in Eden, all she ate was fruit and vegetables since the animals were never killed.

"Why do you kill the animals?" she asked Gilmos with her head down, and her voice softer than usual, a slight hint of pain in it.

"We eat meat to give us strength. My mother told me that when man was kicked out of Eden, Anu, and the other Gods told us of meat and how it would help us be stronger. Before that, we were not so different from you fey, according to the stories she told me." he explained to Arwen.

"In any case, getting back to the Pork chops, which we will be eating for dinner, not breakfast, there are a few preparations for them." Gilmos showed Arwen the salt, white sugar, brown sugar, black pepper, ginger, garlic, rosemary, bay leaves, and oranges.

"That's a lot of ingredients," Arwen said, looking at all of them. "First, put the sugar and black pepper in the bowl with water," he said to her.

"Now you will mix the orange, rosemary, and garlic together with bay leaves and add that to the mix from before," Gilmos said to Arwen. Arwen followed the king and blushed lightly when he took her hand to help her stir everything together. Tamako brought out a bowl of water for the meat to be in before mixing the spice in. Tamako rolled his eyes before exiting the kitchen. Tamako did not understand this new emotion he was having when seeing the two laughs together and enjoy one another's company.

"Thank you, Tamako," said Gilmos before Tamako left. Tamako would normally be polite to say thank you but said nothing.

"Now we let this set for four to six hours," he said to Arwen as they added the meat to it.

"You're very knowledgeable in this art of cooking," Arwen said to him.

"It's something I can say my mother taught me in our short time together, and she took full advantage of her position to learn from as many chefs as possible, which is one advantage of being royalty," he said with a calm chuckle.

"Thank you for the lesson," Arwen said to the king in a happy tone.

That evening, Arwen tried the meat that the king taught her to spice. She was amazed it was no longer pink but a fine brown, and the taste was amazing. They had lots of vegetables on the side of the dish as well. They enjoyed their meal together. Arwen was a little shocked it was just the two of them that evening. The king had a surprise of light-colored wine as well. "This will not drug you, I promise. I did not pick anything too heavy for a flower such as yourself. It's just a white wine of Lilly, but I will eventually get you to try a glass of red wine," he said, teasing her.

The two enjoyed dinner, and Arwen fell asleep on the king's shoulder. He carried her to her bed, kissed her forehead, and as she rolled to the corner, covered her up in the blue silk blankets.

Chapter 15:

The King went horseback riding

"If you do well at this, I will show you the dragons, later, sense they are much harder to master or tame then the might of the mares and stags" Gilmos said to Arwen "I think I will do just fine, I am not a stranger to animals or mystical creatures" she said with a smirk as she allowed the king to lead the way. The two went to the fields with the horses. Arwen rode a white Lipizzan horse whose main was long and soft as silk and Gilmos sat astride a black one that was a Murgese. Gilmos choice of horse hair was more fluffy and excellent to be braided in fine gold beads less wavy and more firm a main. They then raced and after Gilmos beat Arwen, she fell into the grass.

"Let me help you," he said trying to help her get the grass out of her hair that stuck in her light purple hair and decorated her with strains of dark green. Arwen grabbed a white flower from the ground. The king took it from her hand taking it playfully from her fine fingers that had graceful long feminine nails. He then stuck the white flower behind her ear.

"The grass does not suit your beauty but this does he said smiling softly.

Chapter 16:

On the seventh hour when a few days past Gilmos showed Arwen the dragons and them road on an enormous golden dragon.

"My Lady, are you enjoying the view?" he asked her in a kind tone.

"Your lady?! I am my own woman, and I do not belong to you or anyone else for that matter. But yes, I am enjoying this view you speak of and the clouds are beautiful and air easy to breathe." Arwen said. Then after the seventh day, their first real adventure had begun.

"Tell me a story or fact regarding the dragons?" he asked her as he took Arwen's hand and stroked the middle of her palm.

"The gods have said the dragons were made from the fires and oceans of the deep. They tell us that there are over the world but that most of the man has either tamed them or hunted them down." Arwen said looking at the king as she pulled her hand away.

"I am going to show you the dragon's barn, I am sure Glory would not mind me showing that to you," Gilmos said to Arwen. Gilmos took the reins of the dragon. Arwen looked up at him a little confused thinking Gilmos had already shown her the dragons. The dragons' barn was on a mountain just outside Babylon. Glory laid her claws in the ground.

"Did you not show me the dragons earlier?" Arwen asked as they got off Glory. Gilmos helped Arwen off the dragon. They walked into the giant barn that was at least two times larger than normal barns. Inside lay, three female dragons curled up around ten eggs. The dragons nested like birds did and a male dragon flew down into the barn bringing in a meal for the female dragons. Arwen walked up to one of the dragon eggs and stroked it.

"The eggs are so rough, and some look very crystalline and others look more scale or rock-like,"

Arwen said as she looked at the eggs and how tiny they were compared to the large dragons that laid them.

"That's because of the different types, we have caught many and given them a sanctuary but here we don't fear them, I suppose despite this being the oldest city, we are ahead of the rest," Gilmos said with a soft smile.

Chapter 17:

The first of their adventures was to kill the Akhkhazu a female three-headed monster whose red, white, and greenheads argued as if they were sisters as opposed to a single entity that kills its enemies with illness and virus. For in Babylon, many of the people had become nauseous and grotesque with sickness. Those infected would become blistered and red and black with great swelling and a rash would appear all over their bodies. The sisters rode on a horse that matched the color of their heads. The first of the sisters, who had red skin covered with feathers, and yellow eyes like a harpy. The second of the sisters was white, her skin looked like a harpy's, but had the beauty of a swan and dark blue eyes. The third sister's skin was snake-like and even her eyes were more reptilian an orange-yellow color. The beast was sent by the enchantress to spread sickness in the land which was killing many in the Kingdom without warning. Most of those who became ill only lived for ten days after that. Arwen rode on a brilliant brown mustang with a white spot on its forehead while the King rode on a jet-black stallion. Tamako had been left in the Kingdom to tend to the sick. Tamako would use steam and oils to help the ill breath. It seemed that everything Tamako did only helped soften their pain rather than cures the infirmed. The King was not thrilled with the idea that this girl was going to help him but as he had warmed up to her some thanks to their encounters before this battle, he had decided that she may be of use. Gilmos, who was known for fighting alone and ruling with an iron fist, did like to show his softer side to anyone especially this girl, Arwen. They rode for some time until they reached a cave. The cave had the scent of blood and decay. The three sisters were staying in their lair deep within the darkness of the cave. Gilmos and Arwen tied their horses to a tree that was just outside the cave and heavy with what appeared to be delicious golden apples.

"We should slit the horse's throat to make sure these monsters have nowhere to run," Gilmos said

"We shall do no such thing King Gilmos! The horse is innocent, it is not the master," Arwen replied.

"We shall cut the rope and let it run free and it will be able to live off all the apple trees in this valley, Anu would want none of the animals harmed unless it were to used for sustenance," Arwen said to Gilmos.

"You listen too much to the God who made you from the earth," Gilmos glared at her. Nevertheless, Arwen cut the ropes and laid her hand upon the horse, calming it, before setting it free.

"A soft hand can solve many problems Lord Gilmos, as I saw you do with those puppies, blood and vengeance are not always the answer," she said to him noticing the disapproving look he gave her

"Yes, but this thing belongs to the enemy and if I show them the mercy they could get away…but I suppose if it will make you happy that I have mercy on them then I shall, my dear," he said rolling his eyes. The two then entered the cave. Arwen held her sword tightly in her hand and Gilmos placed his back to her back so they could protect each other.

"Sisters, do you see what I see?" said the first sister.

"Yes, I see, I see," said the second sister."

"Dinner came to us today, sisters," hissed the third sister The sisters came from all three sides laughing loudly as they drew closer to Arwen and the King, they knocked Arwen down with their tale.

"Have I caught myself a little fey to eat today?" said the first sister as she saw Arwen fall to the ground. While they were distracted, Gilmos snuck up and struck the snake-like sister on the neck cleanly severing her head as the other two sisters screamed in agony and recoiled in pain.

"Get back beastly, flesh rotting demon," he said. The blood dripped down his blade as the snake-like head of the reptilian sister fell to the floor. Then the red sister attempted to superheat the King's sword, using fire magic. After a moment the blade of the King's sword glowed a bright orange from the magic

"Burn! Burn demi-God! No one to save the mistake of the Goddess of the herd" the redhead of the beast said as she cast her spell upon the weapon

Arwen, noticing that the ground was wet and had several puddles of water on it began to chant and used the water to cool off the king's blade

"Goddess of the seas, I ask you to lend allow me the use of your water," she chanted as the water began to undulate as though dancing to unheard music. Then as one, they took down the remaining two sisters, one of whom was very pale and released a high-pitched scream, as she died.

"Not a bad fight…, but I could have beaten those three on my own quite easily without your help, little one," Gilmos said

"You should be grateful rather than present such strong-willed and harsh words King Gilmos" Arwen replied. It was then that she realized she was attracted to the King, despite the harshness of his words.

Chapter 18:

Later that evening, after the two had returned to the fortress, Arwen realized she was very tired and returned to her chambers.

"Lord Anu…. The King confuses me, he has kindness but chooses to hide it" Arwen explained as she spoke into the necklace that Anu had given her.

"Will you stay then to help him be true to himself and stop Inu?" asked Anu.

Arwen laid her head back on the pillow; thoroughly enjoying the silk pajamas she was allowed to wear though it had only been a few months since she came here, the castle was starting to feel like home. She did miss Eden and all the birds that sang there. The earth had birds as well but the birds held a different note and sound to them.

Arwen never noticed that she acted a bit more human than fey she closed her eyes then opened them.

"Anu I will stay…. but why does Inu want to destroy this King if he is your blood? I don't understand, what does she want war?" she asked inquisitively.

"I made a mistake Arwen, and made a deal that I should not have, I should have considered Gilmos would want to find love on his own and in his way," Anu explained.

"I thought Gods were perfect…." She said taken aback at this revelation.

"Even Gods make mistakes and can die. Our immortality has limits and weaknesses. I made a mistake because I bargained with the Gods of chaos and the underworld so that my grandson could come to Eden, that was my daughters wish and the more I think about it the more I think perhaps Ninsun was right, maybe for the family, I should have broken the rules. I put my duties above my family." Anu said the pain in his voice evident

"Then…, why did you not? You are the ruler of all the gods," she spoke though she was not one to question any of the Gods she was starting to see that she was allowed to think

for herself.

"The world is a delicate thing, and if I broke my rules

that are set order would be lost. It seems the very thing I was

trying to prevent is going anyway and it seems order is lost

now. Sweet flower child, you are fixing my mess," Anu said to

Arwen. Arwen then closed the crystal and drifted off into a

deep sleep. She dreamt of the world she left and wondered if

she made the right choice.

Chapter 19:

Gilmos decided he would surprise the fey girl with a gift. Gilmos had the palace decorated with bright red roses. Arwen was confused by that action as well.

"I thought roses were a romantic gesture…and I am not romantically interested in him; I am just a fey on a mission," she said as she walked the hallways thinking the King likely had a possible queen to be arriving. She looked for Tamako to explain to her why the castle was filled with flowers.

"Um Tamako, is the King expecting someone," she asked him curiously.

Tamako wondered if he should spill the King's reason behind it or if it was not for him to say.

"I am not sure my lord would want me answering that, but perhaps, he just thought you were homesick since Eden has so many flowers" Tamako explained to her.

Arwen picked up a few rose petals off the floor

"You told me men only use flowers for the act of courtship so if that is true then that means…." Arwen blushed lightly but quickly brushed it off.

"Aw Tamako, I told you to tell me when my lady had arisen," Gilmos said smiling. Arwen looked at the King's dark brown eyes and for once tried her best not to make contact with them.

"Lord Gilmos what is all this for…." she asked not wanting to jump ahead of what it could mean.

"This is for the celebration of our victory against the three sisters and to our future battles, would you like some wine," he asked her kindly as one of his servants brought out a tray of wine

"If we have more battles to face, is now really the time for celebration?" Arwen asked as she took some of the rose red-colored wine and put the silver jewel-encrusted goblet to her lips. Arwen was uncertain if the King a classy man or was he simply trying to lure her into his bed, but in any case, she felt there was no time for distractions or emotions. Tamako found it interesting, that though Arwen was drawn to the gifts the King offered, she did not express the same level of interest the other women seemed to. Tamako could tell there was something about her that might be good for the King overall but he was uncertain if that's what he wanted because just as the King had taken an interest in the little fey, so had he. He had also noticed a spark in the King that he had not seen since before the King's mother had passed on.

Chapter 20:

The peaceful quiet in the Kingdom was not destined to last long as the next on Inu's monsters had descended upon it. Gilmos had decided he would ready his armies to take down the small monsters whilst he and Arwen took care of the big ones. Their next enemy was the scorpion people. The scorpion people were known for serving the sun God Utu. When Arwen had heard who it was, she wondered why so many Gods were starting to side with Inu. She was worried that if this continued, the other Gods would also turn against Anu and not just try to take His Grandson's kingdom, Babylon.

"The scorpion people serve Utu," Arwen said as she looked towards Gilmos.

"I told you and my people the Gods cannot be trusted!" he spat at Arwen, silently willing himself not to tell her of the dreams he had been having where he saw his mother warning him of something.

"Tell the men to cut the tails of the scorpion people off and to try not to let their stingers catch any of them" he explained. The Soldiers went into a period of training wherein they used soft pillows and wire to make fake tails that one soldier would wear while the other try and cut it off. The King was being a bit more standoffish during this time than usual, which allowed everyone, including Arwen, to see he was tense about the coming battle

"I have an idea; what if we use the horses to gain some higher ground and rocks to knock them down before they can reach the top of the castle walls?" Arwen said trying to be supportive.

Gilmos liked the idea and so they began to build weapons that could break the shells of the enemy, while the mapmakers in the Kingdom began to figure out the best place to set each of the creations that could do this.

Gilmos wanted to make sure as few of his men would be in close combat with those things as possible.

"Ready my armor," Gilmos ordered "Arwen and I will go after the two main scorpions," Gilmos said

"Would it not be better for you to stay in the royal residence walls and let someone else handle the big ones," asked one of the men.

"No, a King's place is at the forefront of the battle, not to worry my best friend is going to help me with the two of them," Gilmos said looking at Arwen, who turned bright red.

"I want Xavier and Damien to guard the left gate. West and Romeo shall guard the right gate" Gilmos said as he began to plan everyone's place of action. Gilmos showed no emotion in his eyes and his voice held confidence despite the stress he was carrying. He accidentally placed his hand on Arwen's when he was moving the men on the map.

"Sorry, I guess I lost sight of where to put this guy," he said moving his hand away and brushing his black curly hair behind his ear.

"It's fine, as you were saying where shall we put the class A, B, C, and D, soldiers," Arwen said getting him back on track. The A-class soldiers were on the east side and the B class ones are to be on the west side that left groups C and D to reinforce the east and west sides of the castle

"Tamako gets me, Yati," he said moving on to the next order of business; where to put the civilians if things did not go according to plan. Yati came into the battle room with a map of the tunnels that were under the city and would Gilmos her plan for all the women and children to be there and have escape patterns in place should the scorpions make their way into the city.

"Do not worry my King, I shall keep the woman and children safe" Yati said to Gilmos as she bowed low

"You seem to have high regard to the woman and children that is very noble of you," Arwen said. She could see that the King's eyes were not glowing as they typically did; as if the light was taken from them making his brown eyes seem darker than normal.

"No one should be without a mother, a mother's song is the sound of safety," Gilmos said. For despite how disrespectful he was, he had a lot of respect for mothers and made it his mission to protect them. Arwen still could not understand why the King kept so much of his emotions hidden. She felt like she was looking at a mask that wanted to break. She had seen what she perceived as cruelty; he had shown no mercy to those who dared to come near his Kingdom or to the common thief on the street. It became clear to Arwen each time she observed the King that the tyrant was a mask and that there was nobility with goodness in his heart. It made her wonder, did Anu do everything in his power to save him because he was kin, or because he knew the King Gilmos could be.

"Then we have our plan ready now remember everyone we do this for the glory of Babylon," Arwen said trying to cheer on the men. Gilmos looked at Arwen as if she was acting like a child yet at the same time, he was drawn to how her positivity seemed to make the men eager to go out there. Gilmos knew that despite the weapons they had made there still be much death for the scorpion men normally guarded relics and chambers of the Sun God. It was out of character for them to be here. This made Gilmos hope that the moon God did not also turn his back on Babylon.

"If it is just the scorpions, we will be able to rest at night for the scorpions cannot fight in the dark," Gilmos explained. The scorpion men could only come during the day and would turn to dust if they were out of their chambers after moonrise. It was just too bad that the moon could not be lit by man. Gilmos would also have to worry about the heat and make sure his men had lots of water.

"Please ensure that all of you have extra water skins, for if you are unable to come back into the walls of the castle, I do not wish to see you die of the heat," Gilmos said.

"Each unit will have seven members assigned to keep track of food and water remember, our goal is to smash them or to have the moon hit them at nightfall," Gilmos said as Arwen began to roll up the maps as everyone went to their posts. She began to remember the moonstones in Eden.

"It's too bad we do not have moonstones. Then we could make weapons that could easily destroy them or even create a protective layer around the city" Arwen said as she played with her crystal around her neck.

"That's not a bad idea but it is very hard to get such a thing and we do not have that kind of time," Gilmos said. They could hear the scorpions as they drew closer to the castle. The scorpion men's shells were gold, yellow, orange, and red, along with a few black ones. The colors of the shells warned their level of poison, with the Gold shelled scorpion men being the least poisonous and the Black shelled ones being the most lethal

"Remember men gold shelled scorpion man has the least potent of the venoms whereas a black shelled Scorpion Man is the most potent, and a red shell will either cause you to feel like your insides are burning or cause you to be trapped in a false fear so be extra cautious lest you end up in a pretty black coffin," Gilmos said to his men. Arwen lightly struck the King's arm showing her disapproval of his words. As Arwen gathered her weapons she was a little worried about an enemy that could poison but also heal in the sun. The odds were not in the King's favor, but she knew that he and his men were going to fight these things to the very end.

"All we have to do is take out the two lead ones and then the rest will scatter like ants," Gilmos said, remembering how his mother used to tell him that the scorpion people followed a leader and that if he could take out the two leaders, they would lose direction.

"I hope that is that simply because there are so many of them," Arwen said.

Arwen and Gilmos followed a river out of the kingdom. The soldiers were all in their formations, waiting for Arwen and Gilmos to give the signal. The signal was going to be made using a mirror to the four points of the Kingdom. One Mirror rested with Arwen and Gilmos as well as with each of the commanders.

"Arwen would you please do me the honor of sending out the signal to the men?" Gilmos said as he stepped back from the light that tricked into the watery area that they stood in. Arwen then used the mirror to reflect the sunlight to let men know it was time. Yati, who was the first to see the signal, pointed his mirror to the direction of West and Romeo. Then West and Romeo signaled Xavier and Damien. Before long, there were four sharp points of sunlight across the battlefield. Everyone was in their positions and had their weapons readied meanwhile Yati, along with the men the King had given him kept the woman and children safe. Arwen then put the mirror away and she glanced at the King signaling him with her hands for them to move out.

"Gilmos, shall I take out that one first, or should we do it together one," she asked him.

"It would be best, my dear, if we took one each otherwise we risk one of them coming from behind," he said to her.

She glared lightly when he said dear and hid her pink cheeks behind her blade trying her best to ignore the compliment

"Very well, I will take out the black one, you take the yellow one, just remember these are super poisons compared to the rest of the kind," he said looking towards her. Arwen nodded her understanding of the risks involved. Arwen had a bow and arrow upon her back, for she had decided that she would not use a sword alone, for this fight. She had tied a rope to the end of one of her arrows with the intent of tripping each of the beasts to make killing them easier for her and the King. As the two Scorpion Men approached them, she fired the rope-laden arrow into the far wall and pulled the rope taught causing the two Scorpion Men to fell upon their backs and as they struggled to regain their footing, Arwen went after the tail of the yellow Scorpion Man. Once the shell fell free of its body, she cut its tail off and then began to cut through the scorpion's yellow shell. The King did the same to the black Scorpion Man though he had a bit more difficult because the Scorpion Man put up more of a fight. The scorpion hit Gilmos in the chest leaving a rather sizable gash across it despite the armor he wore, fortunately, Gilmos was a Demi-God.

"Gilmos!" Arwen shouted as she saw the wound on the King standing over the body of the now-deceased Scorpion Man, which covered in blood, some of which was Gilmos'. She ran to his side and placed her arm under his to help the king walk It was obvious from the huge black and purple bruise in addition to the gash that the king was in pain.

"We need to get you to the palace right away. Arwen said concerned. The scorpion men were already starting to scatter as their two leaders had been killed there were a few stragglers who had minds of their own, so Arwen fought through them the best she could along with some of the other men. She finally made her way to one of the gates Xavier and Damien were stationed at. The two men took Gilmos from Arwen's arms as they had noticed that she was struggling to carry the King because he weighed far more than what she could carry on her own. The King, thanks largely to his divine blood, was still awake despite the intense pain. When they made their way into the hall, they noticed West laying there bleeding and several other men also injured from the attack.

"Did… we win, Lady Arwen?" West asked breathing hard and almost passing out as his eyes started to close. Arwen had never seen so much bloodshed. She went to the broken soldier and whispered in his ear.

"Yes, we did, they're scattering now, only a few remain who think on their own, rest easy now West," she said pulling away from the soldier's hand she then made her way to the where the king lay injured.

Chapter 21:

"You don't need to worry about me Arwen. The blood I hate, the same blood that flows through me, will only have me in bed for a week or two. We will double the guards. That should take care of the stragglers," he said looking up at her. At that point Tamako entered the chambers and pulled the girl away so the King could rest; his injuries were not as bad as the other men who went head-on with those creatures. Tamako seemed off somehow though and Arwen noticed he had a red fire like a pendant around his neck that was similar to the communication crystal that she wore. She saw Tamako whisper something to two of the servant girls.

"Thank you, Tamako, but I think I will sleep on the floor of his bed-chamber till he is fully covered," she said looking at Tamako. The tone of her voice held a deep concern for the King. She did not know why but she could feel some sort of tension there as Tamako's dark blue eyes met with her light blue eyes and she saw that his brown hair was frizzled. She tried not to read too much into it because maybe it was just the tension of the recent battle Arwen tended to the King's wounds every day for two weeks. The King was happy with this and was a little shocked she would do so much for him.

"Why are you taking care of me, don't you know that that is my servants and concubines' job?" he said with a chuckle as he placed his hand on hers as she was redressing his wounds. Arwen let out a heavy sigh

"I do it not because of Anu if that's what you are thinking, but because I can tell your people need you just like nature in Eden needs the fey to take care of it," she said looking into his brown eyes. The King leaned closed to her attempting to kiss her but failing as she pulled away from and pushed his hand away from her hand.

"Why not use your magic to heal me? I always thought fey were known for their healing powers, dearest" Gilmos said flirting somewhat with Arwen.

"You are a Demi-God, and as such you are healing just fine, the fey powers should only be used in an extreme emergency besides there is a trade-off, when we fey heal another it takes from our life force and though our lives are longer than that of man we dare not play with them," she explained rolling her eyes to him and ignoring the compliment.

"Lay by my side, I promise I won't bite," he said to her as he patted a space on his bed.

"Fine but only for a moment," she said as she lay down beside him and was immediately ensconced by his arms.

"I don't think friends should be this close, and you should know that is as far as this is going," she said so he did not get any ideas to try and make any move on her. Just then, the King's jester and advisor came into his chambers.

"Am I interrupting, Lord Gilmos?" Tamako asked as an angry look crossed his now well-groomed features, he had come to teach Arwen some more about how humans worked.

"No, no, Tamako, why the angry look on your face you used to be so calm and cheerful," Gilmos said to him.

"I am alright, I just thought you would want to know, my lord, that we have received information on the Enchantress' next move and where her lair might be," Tamako said to the King. Arwen moved out from under the King's arms and brushed off her dress a little embarrassed to be seen acting like a woman, lest she is seen as vulnerable

"I should probably contact Anu and let him know these new findings, I will go get dressed in my training gear," she said slightly flustered.

"The dress looks nice on you, you should relax more often," Tamako said looking at her then away from her.

"Thank you," she said as she went off to her quarters to change and to contact Anu so that she could apprise him of the current situation.

Chapter 22:

Arwen still did not understand why the Gods were doing what they were doing when Inu had no right to do the things she was doing. She could not lose faith in Anu or Urus.

Arwen made her way to the training room and had begun to polish one of the blades when her mentor stepped in with a new weapon in hand.

"Let's try spears today, after the battle with the scorpions I think the King would prefer weapons that could be used at a distance," He said tossing one to her after she put the blade back on the wall with the other swords, there were also other weapons including bows, spears, slingshots, axes, and maces, as well as shields and armor which was something most Kingdoms were lucky to have a few of. Babylon however was fortunate not just a few shields and suits of armor, but they, in fact, had several shields and suits of armor

"Then why not archery? It too allows for ranged combat and I used it in the last battle," She asked curious about the schedule change. To her, it felt like Tamako was just trying to get her away from the King but for what reason? She did not think Tamako would ever hurt her or the King but she had seen a shift in his behavior; he used to be kind to everyone in the Kingdom and lately his attitude was getting as bad as the Kings. Still, with her he was soft most of the time except training wherein he was hard on her because he was attempting to make her a better fighter

"Do it again, never allow your enemy to get that close" he said crossing his arms as he watched one of the soldiers was sparring with her. He then placed his hand up letting the soldier know to stop the session.

"You're getting lazy little duck, how about you face me now," he said. Arwen had not faced Tamako since the first time she had come into the Kingdom and she had lost then and was handed to the King as she recalled her very first rude encounter with the two men. It was clear the memory distracted her. Tamako struck her, knocking her into the wall and down he placed his hand on her wrist causing the staff to slip from her hand as he kissed her. Arwen then kicked his, ankle knocking him down. As the King walked in on the training session, he could tell by the look on Arwen's face something was bothering her. The King did not see the advance Tamako had made.

"Arwen, are you alright?" he asked for once not adding a dear or my lady because he did not wish to upset her more.

"I'm fine…" she said upset biting her lip slightly trying to understand the rudeness the humans seemed to have towards females her body langue showed she was not fine. As the two men began to argue, Arwen stomped off.

Chapter 23:

She was puzzled as to why Tamako would be so disrespectful he was always polite and asked for everything. She had always liked that about him over how arrogant the King could be. Tamako was the first friend she had made in the Kingdom. He had taught her everything she knew about humans and got her to see the King for who he was. In many ways, Tamako was one of her dearest friends in the kingdom.

"Am I the reason they're fighting?" she wondered. She put on a brown cape to hide her pointy ears and She mounted one of the horses and rode towards one of the fountains in the city

"Lord Anu always warned me mankind lusted for the fey. Does the King have feelings for me? I refuse to be the reason this Kingdom falls apart" tears fell from her eyes, both the King and Tamako had become dear to her. She did not want to have to pick between them but she feared that that day would come. A little old woman came up to her offering her an apple.

"Why do you cry?" the old woman asked.

"I am sorry, I should not be crying in public like this, I am just worried about the King that's all," she said wiping the tears from her eyes and accepting an apple from the old lady

"I knew the King's mother, long ago, the boy was happy then, and Tamako was raised beside him though the King did not age like the rest of us, neither has Tamako, legend says that the King's mother gave up her immortality for him but no one knows how Tamako has kept his youth…so strange, your hair is purple you must be fey" the woman with her little walking stick.

"I am but let's not talk about that right now," Arwen said holding a finger up to her lips. She had begun to wonder why Tamako was different just like her and the King.

"Might I ask your name please?" she asked not wishing to be rude to the old woman who had just given her fruit and given her useful information. "My name is Octavia," she said to Arwen.

"Tell me how does one become more than a normal human if not a Demi-God or fey or some other sort of mystical creature?" Arwen asked the old woman.

"Either they possess great strength, magic, or blessed by the Gods, Tamako was for the King marrying Inu, but the King thought Inu would bring hardships to us, but, no woman likes to be turned down," the old woman said.

Chapter 24:

Arwen helped the woman back to the Kingdom and made her way back to the castle where she checked on the King and Tamako. She was curious as to how Tamako was able to stay young. She decided she would confront him later and depending on his answers, she would let the king know what she had found out. She did not wish to worry about the King for nothing. She noticed something odd in the castle regarding the stingers from the scorpions they had killed their poison was being saved but the men would not say who gave that order. Arwen found that strange as well and also felt that was something she should bring to the King's attention. She started to write down all the strange things she noticed. That night she finally made her way to Tamako's chambers to confront him.

"Tamako, May I ask you a personal question?" she said trying not to make it obvious she still felt uneasy being around him after what he tried.

"I'm sorry about earlier, I meant no offense, and yes ask away, I must serve the King and answer your questions," he said acting more like his old self.

"A villager told me you are as old as Gilmos and that like him you do not age normally how is this?" she asked as she looked at him. Tamako placed some of Arwen's purple hair behind her ear making her jump. He then withdrew, returning to his old manners.

"My father made a deal with the Enchantress when I was a boy; my father would kill for her and in return, his son would not age, till the death of the King," Tamako said to her. Arwen was not sure if she should believe him. That night Arwen asked the King to allow the old woman to stay a few days which he allowed though he felt like questioning why, he decided that Arwen's happiness was more important, which baffled him because he had never really cared for another individual aside from Tamako

Chapter 25:

That night Tamako used the red crystal he wore to communicate with Inu, in the same fashion as Arwen had with Anu

"I have done as you have asked Lady Inu. Do me a favor and just keep your end of the bargain, don't harm the girl," Tamako said looking into the red crystal.

"My my, I don't intend to my dear sweet bat, you just make that toxin and do not strike until I tell you, and not a moment sooner, remember you must mix it with the purple iris, the black widow's poison, the scorpion's venom, and the gorgon's tears," she said as she played with her red hair. Tamako was beginning to have second thoughts about what the two were planning, still, he had grown quite close to the girl, and a part of him was jealous. He found himself thinking back to the talk he and Gilmos had had before the King had been wounded

"It will be done Enchantress Inu," he said cutting off the communication and closing his eyes. Tamoko took the purple flowers with their yellow powder and crushed them down. He took off the legs of the black spider his eyes looking sharply on the deep red icon so well known to that breed of spider. He took the stinger and squeezed out as much of the poison as he could. He then pulled out the vial of Gorgon tears the enchantress had provided for him. His face was filled with pain and guilt for the deed he was doing. He let out a deep sigh as he pushed his brown hair back from his forehead as he looked deeply into the purple-green liquid. When he placed the spoon in the mixture to stir the concoction, his mind wondered. Mentally, he traveled back to the time when the King was telling Tamako his new feelings towards Arwen.

"Tamako can I trust you with my newest interest," the King asked. "Let me guess, you have a new possible queen or love interest," he asked raising his eyebrows.

"More like old as she has been with us for some time now. It would not be an affair but a permanent member of the castle. It's Arwen, after the war, I want to ask her to be my queen. My problem is that I know not which ring to pick. It is hard to decide which ring would suit her eyes or even what wedding dress would best suit her," he explained.

"My lord does a bride not pick their dress. In any case, Gilmos, Arwen is not like other women. Do you even think she wants what a human woman wants? Not to be rude my lord, but why don't you just bed her and be done with it?" Tamako said making it clear that he wanted to change the subject

"She is different, I would rewrite the stars if she commanded it, you're not jealous, are you?" he said to Tamako as he noticed Tamako cross his arms.

"No, no, I just think Anu would want his grandson to marry more than a fey, after all, fey is born to work for the Gods so they are servants like myself," Tamako said hoping to get the Kings interest elsewhere.

"That's why she's a perfect fit for a Demi-God," Gilmos said gesturing to himself.

"Would you not prefer a princess of some other Kingdom, to join and expand your Kingdom?" he said as a final attempted to get the King to change his mind. "Don't be silly Tamako, my choice, is always best for my Kingdom, and the people love her," Gilmos said "I have some jobs to do, will talk more later friend," Tamako said walking away. Tamako then opened his eyes as the memory ended. He never thought he'd fall for the same woman as the King had, but it happened. He was going to prepare everything like he was instructed. The only question that remained was would he be able to carry out his nefarious deed or would he end up choosing what he has always known over what he had not. Tamako had been a servant all his life that is how he would live and die. If he did it, he had to hope Arwen would never find out the truth or she would hate him for it but at the same time if he did not there was a strong possibility, she would pick the King and not him. He also understood there was a possibility she would pick neither and travel the human world like she originally intended to. Tamako got the clothes for the female shapeshifter the enchantress had sent; little did he know that enchantress herself was going to come.

Chapter 26:

He then went to find Arwen as it was time for her daily lessons.

"Let's have you teach me today, and then you can go hang out with the King," Tamako said to Arwen as they went to a garden where there were many flowers laid out with paper and pen beside them

"Tell me the meaning of each of the six flowers and then I want you to tell me what they are most often used for," Tamako said looking at her and hoping he was doing a better job of hiding the guilt he felt than he thought he was.

"The first three flowers are the roses, and the yellow one means friendship, while the white rose represents purity, and the red rose represents passion and love," she said looking at him then she moved on to the next three flowers.

"The Iris despite its beauty and the amazing scent is highly venomous, they stand for hope, trust, royalty, and victory. She said looking at them

"Now which flower do you think best suits me?" he asked her as she walked around the flowers.

"You Tamako are like the yellow rose a friend who brings joy into people's lives. I think that if it was not for you and the King, I would not fit in here." She said to him.

"What flower would you use for the King?" he asked, not entirely certain he wanted to hear the answer.

"That's rather hard I feel like he is a white or purple rose or maybe even a red rose, not that I am in love with him or anything but he is very passionate about his Kingdom," she said placing her hands in front of her face in an attempt to hide her flustered bright red cheeks.

Chapter 27:

A few days had passed and Tamako was a little disappointed in the last time he interacted with Arwen. He did not understand why she favored the King over him and the rejection pushed him to make the tea with the fatal toxin the enchantress had told him about. Tamako placed the poison in a dark purple cup and the tea that did not have poison in a green cup. He then had a few other cups on the tray in case Arwen and the King had others with them. Tamako carried the tray of cups to the dining hall where a small fire was alight in the fireplace in the center of the room. He then handed the tray to a servant girl. The servant girl's hair was a fine red, but it was unnoticed by the inhabitants of the castle, including those in this very room. She had disguised herself and used glamour spells so no one could see her true form. She placed the green cup near the King and the purple cup near Arwen. Arwen then brought the purple cup to her lips and took a sip, after which she began to feel very sick and began to cough up some blood and she placed her hand to her neck trying to breathe but though her lungs ached for air, she simply could not breathe and her other hand clutched at her chest. Arwen eventually lost consciousness. The King held the girl in his arms as tears filled his eyes as he kissed her, hoping that his kiss would revive her like in the stories his mother had told him when he was a boy

"That was a little too easy," Inu said as she lifted the glamour spell. The King lifted his head at the familiar voice and when he saw who was speaking, he clenched his fists in anger

"Don't look so surprised pet, did you think I was going to let the competition live," she said looking with a smirk, believing her victory was at hand. The King looked to where Tamako was as he lifted her from the floor placed Arwen onto the table, Gilmos noticed that she was breathing weakly.

"Tamako, get the guards immediately!" Gilmos shouted, angrier than he had ever been before

"You call for help from the man who created the poison?" she said now wearing a dark black dress in place of the servant's clothes she once wore

"What…did you do, Tamako?" Gilmos said grabbing a sword from one of the guards. The guards went after the enchantress.

"Guess this is my time to fly like a bird and beat this castle-like the wind," she said leaving in a puff of smoke. Tamako got a sword as he pushed one of the guards. Damien and Xavier grabbed Tamako's arms to cuff them.

"No, let him go, I will deal with his betrayal now, take Arwen to the handmaidens and see if they can save her," Gilmos said barely containing his rage. As Damien let go he looked at Xavier not sure what the King was doing was wise.

"My King, perhaps Tamako was under a spell," they said looking at each other in disbelief of what was transpiring.

"I don't care if he was under a spell, Tamako and I are going to fight to the death," Gilmos said, the rage evident in his eyes

"I am truly sorry, My Lord, the poison was never meant for her I swear," Tamako said feeling so ashamed and guilty about his part in what had happened to Arwen that he was unable to look the King in the eye. Tamako raised his sword and began to defend himself though he did not wish to fight, the King, was more worried about Arwen but he would defend himself, even if it was poorly. Gilmos pierced Tamako's heart. Tamako managed to stab the King near his left rib but it was not deep as Gilmos had penetrated him. As Gilmos pulled the blade out of his body, he felt some sorrow at killing a man he once called his friend and who he once thought was his loyal servant. Gilmos then ran to where Arwen was to check on her. "Is she alright..." he asked the three handmaidens and Octavia, who had joined them in their efforts to heal the little fey. "The leeches are pulling out the poison but it does not look bright my lord," said the handmaiden Lee.

Octavia lifted her guise which was also a glamour spell, revealing her true identity of Ninsun. Gilmos was shocked by what he saw in front of him.

"Mother is that you?? But I saw you die...how can this be?" he said shakily, unsure if he was seeing what his eyes told him he saw

"Unfortunately, I cannot stay long, this is a gift to you from Nergal, he informed me, that this little fey will one day make her journey to his realm but it is not her time to die. Nergal no longer wants to abolish the pact he made with Enil, though he is the God of death and it becomes lonely in his realm as souls come and go, he says too many have died before their time. I have been allowed one year here and I have an antidote for the enchantress' poison," She explained to Gilmos with a smile Gilmos was still unsure whether this was his mother, so he asked her a question that only his mother would know the answer to.

"If you are my mother, tell me about the small hut we passed when I was a child, and whose house did, I mistake it for?" Gilmos asked her as he took the elixir from her hands wondering if this was another trick from the Enchantress or a gift from Nergal. Nergal was not known for his kindness.

Though he did recall his mother saying to him as a child that when Nergal was a young God he was kind and had fallen in love with the Goddess of spring, whom his mother was friends with since one was responsible for the plants the other the animals that man would eat.

"The house was purple and you thought it belonged to the purple fairy that your father's ancestors wrote about," she said to him. Gilmos pulled away rubbing his chin as he processed what she said then quickly handed the elixir to the handmaiden Lee.

"That's correct… and then I stopped there every day hoping to see a purple fairy but one never came," he said reflecting on the memory of his childhood. When Arwen was given the elixir, her face began to regain some color and she coughed a little as her lungs gulped down air. Her eyes began to open as she lifted her head and looked around a little confused about what happened.

"What happened? Gilmos, where are Octavia and Tamako?" she asked feeling better with each passing moment.

Gilmos did not want to answer that though he felt he was in the right on how to handle a traitor. He let out a deep breath as he looked at the woman in the room.

"Octavia is not Octavia but the dead Goddess Ninsun my beloved mother, who has been in the prison of the dead for far too long, sadly she can't stay," he said looking at Arwen glad she would get to meet his mother. He did not know how long she had been here or how much time he had left. When he was a child, he had taken for granted the time with his mother, and for being a prince was often made fun of by the other children of the court and village. He had few friends in Tamako and Lee who had both grown up alongside him. Lee was a fey like Arwen and Tamako's father was a Jester and like Tamako was working with the Enchantress unbeknownst to the court. The three of them never really fit in with the other children especially when they were aging slower on top of having titles though they were workers in the castle.

"If Nergal had shown mercy, then Anu was right again that he would come around with time," Arwen said calmly she tried to get out of the bed still feeling a little lightheaded.

"You need to rest, you both must prepare to face the great Bull of the moon Goddess, this is the last enemy that guards the enchantress' lair," Ninsun told the two as Gilmos caught Arwen and helped her back into her bed medical bed.

Chapter 28:

The enchantress soon learned that just as Tamako had betrayed Gilmos, Nergal had betrayed her and her father Enlil. She was not happy about this at all and contacted her father immediately.

"Father, they keep killing all my pets, tell me how I can get the King or kill him if I cannot have him for myself," she asked petting the Bull of the moon which the moon Goddess Nanna allowed her to borrow.

"Do not worry my clever daughter. If they should kill the bull, Arwen will die. You see, Nanna loves that bull as if it were her child. It is known to the Gods as the bull of the heavens, rather than the bull of the moon as the mortals call it. Though it was not Anu who created it," Enlil explained hoping that this makes Inu be a bit more patient

"Very well father. I will wait and let Nanna kill the girl, and then the King will have to pick me and if not, at least he won't have what he loves most of all," Inu said brushing her long red to the side and pinning up her outfit which was silver with gold lining.

Chapter 29:

After some time passed Arwen, was fully recovered from the toxin she had ingested. She was back to her old self. Arwen's hair was tied back in a braid and she got on a white horse and Gilmos got on his black stallion. The two rode off to the cave where the Enchantress' lair was believed to be. The front of the cave was beautiful and laced with several different stones and crystals: celestine, diamond, apophyllite, amethyst, apatite, chrysocolla, agate, and many others. It looked as if there was a rainbow in the cave which was due to the light reflecting off of the crystals and stones. In the center of the cave was a pool of water beside which sat a bull that was ten times bigger than a normal bull. Its skin was made of fine white crystals but despite its beauty, it was not an innocent creature and very violent when commanded.

"It's a shame that we have to kill it; it's so beautiful and it's not doing any harm, it's just doing its job looking after the moonstones," Arwen said with sadness in her voice as she looked at Gilmos.

"Regrettably, much like a bee though it does good things for the flowers it will sting those who don't let it do its job or that enter into its space.," Gilmos explained. Arwen snuck up to the bull as she preferred to end the beast quietly and peacefully rather than loudly and violently. The bull, however, felt Arwen's hand go on one of its horns and it reacted violently. It got up and nearly tossed Arwen to the side of the cave but she managed to jump on its back. The bull continued to buck wildly in a desperate attempt to throw the fey off it.

"We have to find its soft spot; our swords won't cut through the diamond-plated skin. Arwen yelled to the King as she kept her hands on the bull's horns and then grabbed the robe, she had near her waist to try and create a way to ring it around the mouth like reins on a horse. Gilmos looked and looked to try and find a soft spot but could not seem to find one.

"Should I look under his belly?" Gilmos asked. Arwen put one of her hands on her forehead. "Yes! Look under the belly though I am not crazy about meat, I would rather not be a meal for this thing," she said. Gilmos slide on his knees as his blades went up and noticed most of the cow had diamond plated skin on its underside as well, save for a spot near its stomach

"Guess we are having steak tonight," Gilmos quipped though he knew that no one was going to eat a bull made of crystals. Arwen got off of the bull.

"Not funny Gilmos this is a special creature made by the Gods and so many are hunted by a man that their numbers lesson every year I take no pleasure in this kill though I understand it is necessary in this case since the bull was going to kill whoever Inu had ordered it to.," she said to him

"I was only joking; I meant no offense, My Lady," he said to Arwen.

"Get cleaned up we will need to go deeper and I don't think walking on crystals covered in blood is a good idea; we wouldn't want any other things to find us before we get where we are going," Arwen said handing the King a change of clothes and walking behind a rock to give the King some privacy.

"You know, I don't care if you look, I am not ashamed of my body, and it's not every day a woman gets to look upon a God in all his glory," he said teasing her. Arwen flustered but did not dare look

"You are not a god, and I am not your woman, one should only share such things with the person they wish to be with for the rest of their life," she said putting the extra clothes they brought onto the rocks.

"But I could be your only if you let me," he said sitting on the rocks covered only from the waist down until he put his tunic on after he jumped down from the rocks

"If I say, yes no other women, only me, do you understand," she said as he came up from behind her placing his arms around her. Arwen let her head rest on his shoulder for a few seconds.

"Only you and I will treat you like a Goddess," he said. "Then I say--" before Arwen could finish what she was going to say, a woman came out from the rocks, looked at the dead bull its blood running into the pool beside which Arwen and Gilmos were in each other's arms.

"You swim in the pool I made for my sweet child of the moon, not only this you do not lay my baby under the dirt so that his bones can become stardust, where is Inu? Have you killed her too? She was the last one to be with my baby The Goddess Nanna had said to them. The Goddess's skin was a dark purple laced with silver. Her hair was done up in a star-like pattern and was several shades of purple and blue. The Goddess wore a crown with a silver moon on it upon her head her fingernails were painted silver and her dress was a sparkly white.

"I don't know where Inu is, we were told that this was her lair and we came to fight her, we never wished to kill your beast but she ordered it to kill us," Gilmos said in an attempt to reason with the Goddess. Nanna, however, was driven insane by the sight of the dead bull, and, Arwen and Gilmos were about to feel her wrath.

"Then you will have to suffer the same did no one tell you, a mother will do anything for their child, oh wait…that's right you're too young to know what your mother said and too young to remember her so you only know what you were told about her," the Goddess said to no one in particular as she thought about that meeting with Anu and the other Gods but Nanna had lost her mind and so her words were like a psycho who had been let loose. This was exactly what Enlil wanted he knew how dear that bull was and he had already lost ground with the God of the underworld so he was desperate to gain more ground for his daughter.

"If you have to kill someone kill me for it was I who killed the beast," Gilmos said doing everything in the power to shift the tide and he pulled Arwen behind him and took up his arms. Nanna began to walk around the cave singing a baby's lullaby, stopping near its body, she picked up the dead bull's head and stroked it.

"Grandmother is here now; I promise I will make the bullies pay," the Goddess said ceasing her lullaby, she looked to the Arwen and Gilmos

"No, I think because you took what matters most to me, I will take what matters most to you. The King who claims to have no weaknesses does indeed have a weakness, otherwise, why to kill a childhood friend over a girl who almost died, they told me," she said spinning in a circle and dancing on the crystal rock ground.

"Arwen…. When I say run, you run," Gilmos knew that they did not have any weapons that could kill a God with them and this could only end one way. Gilmos picked up his double blades and would just try and by time for Arwen to getaway. Gilmos felt stupid for not bringing extra men with him he thought he and Arwen would be enough he did not anticipate the two of them had walked in a trap and would be like a mouse and cat. The Goddess was creating sharp crystals from the walls. Gilmos was doing his best to block them with his swords. The crystals were sharper than the blades and were slowly cracking through the blades.

"Let me help, you," Arwen said going to go get the shields from the horse while she did her best to dodge the crystals. Arwen made it back to the King with the shields but even the shields were starting to crack.

"Why must you always be so selfless Arwen I told you to run," he said to her.

"Crack and break like the moon to the sun, crack and break like the sky rocks hit the earth" the moon Goddess was saying; her mind was so far gone.

"I'm not leaving you, no matter what you tell me, we can get past her and find Inu," Arwen said to the King as they tried their best to keep the Goddess at bay finally the shards broke the last shield and Arwen pushed the King aside allowing the silver crystal to hit her.

"I won't allow you to die for me, save your Kingdom and your people and enjoy your mother, bring her a mouse and bear made of wood," Arwen said smiling as the shard cut extremely deeply and she started to bleed. The Goddess sat on the ground picking up rocks

"Pretty, drops of flowers, pretty are the drops of flower child" the rocks were covered in Arwen's blood. A reaper, who was dressed in all black and purple, came out from a shadow portal to collect the soul of the bull.

"Better hurry or I will have to collect her as well, you don't have much time," the reaper said to Gilmos.

Chapter 30:

"Tell the death God to bring back my baby please, please, why do you interfere, the mortal should die for taking my baby," The Goddess said to the reaper. The reaper picked up his scythe.

"Nanna the rules are clear; no God or Goddess may kill a fey or attempt to for they are the gifts of Anu to his wife Urus, Goddess of the earth, but it is also true no fey shall kill nor help kill a beast keyed by the heavens, you Nanna, do not have claim over the dead and it will be Nergal who decides who should live or die.," the reaper said to the distraught Goddess as two fey soldiers appeared and handcuffed her so that she could be taken before the council of the Gods. They took the Goddess of the moon through a portal to Eden where Anu convened the council; however, the only God who did not attend the council meeting was Enlil. Anu was not pleased with this.

"I understand we Gods have not always agreed on the rules but there are rules in place for all of the living things to live the best lives they can in their short time. It is rare when we must put a God or Goddess on trial for crimes and if you the council find her guilty then she will be stripped of her Godhood and most of her power including her immortality and some point in the future her powers and duties will be given to a new deity until then, however, a different God will be temporarily assigned the duties Nanna was given." Anu explained to the council and they all took a seat as some of the fey brought them all drinks and food. Anu and his wife sat at the head of the table.

"I will vote last so as not to influence the vote," Anu said to the council, and with that, the trial began

"I vote guilty, though the bull was killed if we were to allow a kill for a kill, we are no better than a killer," Urus said.

"I agree with Urus, though waters were filled with blood I am certain my fish did not want more of it," Enki said

"This is my sister, so my vote is not guilty of what would the sun be without the moon" Utu answered as he looked toward his sister. The two did not always see eye to eye but he could not bear the thought of her not being among the Gods and in the land of mortals.

"I agree with my husband she polluted the waters with more blood so I vote guilty," Tiamat said.

"I vote not guilty, she had a right to the fey's blood for helping with the kill, and nothing is ever fair in war," Marduk said

"My vote is guilty, she does not decide who lives and dies; that is my job," Nergal said.

"My vote is guilty, for breaking our laws. Your punishment, Nanna is that you will be stripped of your Godhood and your duties will be given to your brother's daughter Diana, you will, however, still be allowed to use the rocks and crystals to help the mortals. You will be the first witch among the mortals, and since I am feeling merciful all of your mortal children can also learn the secrets of the rocks and crystals. When you are old you will be known as the crone," Anu said to Nanna as he cast her to what would be North America in the far future. When Nanna was stripped of her

Godhood her skin turned a dark brown color which resembled what would come to be known as a Native American, the only thing that stayed in place to show her former Godhood was her now normal colored hair which had a few patterns of blue in it that looked like highlights. The council then spoke about what would be Arwen's fate. The Gods agreed that they would let Gilmos try and get her back from the underworld as a test to see if he loved her as he had claimed one day. Anu showed the Council a scene wherein Gilmos appeared to be professing his love to Arwen so that they would better understand his ruling. Arwen wore a blue dress and the chamber windows were adorned with red and gold drapes. The two were eating fruit and wine and talking to each other about their adventures.

"I say if we die, we show the Gods that we would do anything for one another," Gilmos said. "I don't think the Gods would like that and they will not be angry that you even think of it," she asked smiling and holding a strawberry to her lips. He then stroked her face softly and lovingly even though they were just friends.

"I would go to the underworld and back for you Arwen, you are my best friend and my heart," he said to her.

"And you are my best friend King of heroes. I will hold you to that, should I die you are to collect my soul, and if you die, I will do the same, and not even the Gods can stop us" she exclaimed happily. The scene ended as the Gods passed judgment on Arwen.

"Even though they are a little disrespectful, this council will allow Gilmos to attempt to rescue Arwen, and you Nergal shall make the rules of this challenge that we will offer my grandson and my most treasured fey," Anu said.

Chapter 31:

Gilmos was racing back to the castle on his horse trying to get Arwen back to the healers in time. His expression was fierce and he was hopeful despite his concern for Arwen. He kept glancing at Arwen as the blood dripped from her tiny frame. Despite the great speed at which they traveled, it took them seven days to make it back to the castle which was time they could not afford to spare. The bleeding had stopped, but the wound would have to be reopened at the castle. The maiden nurses tried their best to keep the bleeding in check. Gilmos felt he needed to confess his feelings as he let out the breath he wasn't aware he been holding he felt a sharp dagger-like pain in his chest. The King's pride caused him to hold back because of the pain it would cause him if she was to die. The heat-ache was one he had not felt since before his mother had passed on Gilmos did not hold many people close to him unless they were in his inner circle and even then they could be cut down if he felt threatened. When Arwen passed on the tenth day of her injury, he was deeply saddened until he learned that Nergal had sent one of the creatures of the dead to Gilmos' castle that night, but instead of a reaper, it was an old man who took him to a boat with his mother.

"Gilmos, Nergal says you have twenty-four hours to find Arwen in the land of the dead and bring her soul back to the surface or she will stay there," the old man said.

"Nergal would also like you to bring the forbidden fruit of the land of the dead to his one love the Goddess of spring. In exchange for this Nergal will let your mother come again on your first child's 1st birthday and of course, the Gods will resurrect Arwen so what say you?" the old man asked.

"I will do it for my future queen and dearest love to my half-god and half-mortal heart," Gilmos said confidently. As Gilmos looked at the blue river that leads into the underworld he knew he was more than willing to go through all ten levels of it to get to Arwen. The first coating was where the heroes stayed; this was the level on which men, who had been heroic in life resided, it there Gilmos saw West again and the two of them hugged. West warned him of the second area which was the Level of forgotten Kings. When Gilmos made it to this second level, he was shocked to see his father in this realm but at the same time did not know his father well since he died when he was so young. When Gilmos' father explained why he was there Gilmos was not happy to be reunited with him. His father did not have to go to the war since Babylon was winning, but he got greedy and had been drunk with power during his battles which ultimately lead to his death. Gilmos and his father played a game of chess and after he had managed to calm some of his rages, Gilmos put his chair up and crossed his arms placing his feet on the table then brought his hand to his chin to listen with a heavy sigh.

"You know my son, the knight and queen are powerful, and do you remember the game from when you were little," he asked Gilmos. "I do but I can't stay and chat thanks for the game, you won't be seeing me again father," Gilmos replied for he had lost all respect in the dead man. Then Gilmos made it to the third level of the underworld where the animals resided. He was greeted by a black lab who was his dog when he was a boy. He followed the dog who barked and ran in the fields of flowers. Gilmos had already used up five hours with the dog and his father and he still had seven more realms to get through.

"I wish I could take you with me boy." He said to the dog as he petted the dog's ears and stroked its belly. The dog panted and stuck his tongue out between his white teeth. Once he said his goodbyes to his beloved pet and friend, he made his way to the fourth realm. The fourth level had the humans who had been good in life but had decided to stay with their families this was where his mother stayed and was returned to by the old man when they entered the first realm. When he watched the families all he could think about was the future he could have with Arwen and how much he wanted that with her for to him she was more precious than any gem. He hoped to be worthy of such a treasure, and he vowed that he would everything in his power to be worthy of her. Gilmos bade his mother farewell and he then made his way to the fifth realm, the realm of sinners. This realm reeked of death and was filled with the screams of its inhabitants, who were made to pay for their transgressions.

Gilmos did stop to free one sinner and give him water and food. He felt bad for those who had to stay in this realm. Just before exiting the realm, he saw Tomako. Gilmos freed him from the chains, which had bound him to a machine that fed him poison which made sense since he had poisoned Arwen when he was living. Gilmos should have left him to his fate, but Arwen had taught him to be merciful. Gilmos wasted even more time taking Tomako to the land of heroes. "Why did you help me Lord Gilmos, I don't deserve it? I do not deserve it, after what I did," he said to the King.

"I did it for Arwen because if I don't make it in time to save her, I think she would be happy to know that I took the time to help a few others," he said to Tomako.

"Take this, you're going to need it Gilmos, this black stone will render the enchantress' powers useless; I had it in case she tried to betray me and give my student my apologies," he said to the King.

"I will rest easy, Tomako," Gilmos replied as he hugged his friend and then his way to the sixth realm, which was where the monsters went. Gilmos did not feel welcome on this level at all and as a result, he spent as little time there as possible, however since all the monsters he had killed were here and remembered him, they made as much trouble for him as they could and tried to delay him as much as possible. Fortunately, Gilmos was still able to get past them quite easily and so he made his way to the seventh realm, which was where the mystical creatures resided. It was here that Gilmos encountered Nanna's bull once more. At first, the bull was frightened to see him and made a bunch of noise and attempted to run away from him. Remembering how Arwen had tamed a horse, he calmed the beast and mounted it which greatly increased his speed and the ease with which he traverses the other realms which were good because he only fourteen hours remaining. Gilmos then reached the ninth realm, the realm of the aquatic creatures. The bull was able to use its powerful legs to carry Gilmos across the waters and to the tenth, and final realm. It was here he finally found Arwen, for this was the realm where the deceased fey resided, it a rather exquisite place which very much resembled Eden. He ran to her and hugged her tightly.

"My Love, I am sorry for not telling you how much you mean to me sooner," he said kissing her passionately.

"I love you too, Gilmos, I think I have a sense the moment I met you; I just could not say it, what are you doing here? Arwen asked as she returned the kiss

"The Gods have given me a chance to rescue you, my dearest, please be my wife after we defeat the enchantress," he said to her.

"I will be your wife under one condition; you ask the Nergal to let us bring the bull back, It is not fair for Nanna to lose everything because of the enchantress," she said to the King.

"I should have known you would say something like that; you're always trying to save the little animals," he said to her.

The two made their way to Nergal's giant castle which was in the realm of monsters. There, they encountered a large three-headed dog that seemed to be guarding the castle. The dog growled at the bull as the trio approached; When Nergal heard his dog growling he came to see who or what had arrived at his palace

"You two had better not kill my dog, especially after I gave the both of you a chance to be reunited," he said.

"Lord Nergal, Gilmos, and I ask your permission to return the heavenly bull to Nanna," Arwen said to Nergal

"I can grant your request, however, it will not be in the way you think, you see it has been dead for far too long, however, what I can do is tell your sweet grandmother to put its soul into…let's say a baby cow, and it will grow and grow to be what it was and you can gift the calf to Nanna in her now human form, but you, will not deliver it yourselves, instead, you will send seven men across the ocean to Nanna so she does not have to spend her mortal life alone so far away from home," he said to them. Gilmos and Arwen agreed to Nergal's offer and placed the Bull's soul in a vial which they took with them

"Now hurry, you have five hours left!" he said to them as they parted company with him. Arwen and Gilmos barely made it back to the surface with five minutes to spare, and once they got there, Arwen regained her physical body. She now had a white and pink streak in her hair, a gift for her second chance at life.

Chapter 32:

They decided they would send the seven men and the calf once their victory had been achieved. Gilmos, having learned from his previous mistakes, got an army as well as some handmaidens who would heal any of the men who got injured ready to accompany him and Arwen to the cave for the final battle with the enchantress. Their total force was 50 including Arwen and Gilmos, and Gilmos hoped it would be enough and so they gathered the items they would need for the coming battle.

The enchantress who was watching these events transpire via her crystal ball was angry yet again. "If they think they can simply come here and defeat me and I will not resist them, they have another thing coming!" she said holding her staff aloft, conjuring an enormous storm. She gathered an army double the size of the army Gilmos was bringing. Though she knew that it would void the deal she had made with Nergal, she decided to bring back some of the dead to aid her in her quest for vengeance

"I call upon the dead, who have sinned and who lay unused, broken Kings and warriors rise and aid me in my quest to destroy the King and his pet," she said as she moved her staff in a circular motion while she continued to chant. The rain began to fall hard on Babylon and for the next seven days, they are greeted with a monster they had to battle. Inu wanted to ensure that by the time they made it to her gates, they would have so few men that she would have the upper hand, or so she thought. The ten maidens did their best to keep the soldiers fighting, while the ten archers kept their bows firing and the ten swordsmen carried with them double swords and daggers which they used with great skill. The last of the frontline troops were the ten strongest gladiators in the kingdom who had been told that if they helped him, the King would grant them their freedom and citizenship of Babylon. Finally, there were ten cannons, five cooks, and five dog handlers at the rear of the army and the cannon did their best to provide artillery support for the Swordsmen and Gladiators. Arwen and Gilmos had full armor on. Gilmos wore a suit of the finest golden armor while

Arwen wore the finest silver armor. The two held hands as they lead their men. They had dog handlers at the front of the army and the maidens in the rear with the cannon and cooks. Knowing that the dogs could pick up on and track the monster's scents, Gilmos ordered them to the front of the army to provide it with advanced notice of any incoming threat

"Men today we do not ride just for Babylon, but for all mankind; the Gods have grown tired of Inu abusing her powers and we shall not, I repeat we shall not allow this to continue are you with me.," he said to his men.

"For Babylon and King Gilmos," the troops said in unison as they raised their weapons towards the skies "Once we have achieved victory, we will have a great celebration, and Arwen and I will be wed!" Gilmos proclaimed.

"All hail future queen, Arwen! Long live our future queen!" the troops cried, again raising their weapons. Gilmos left the kingdom on High Alert and had ordered that all the markets be closed and all families stay inside their houses while he and Arwen went to fight the enchantress. They even packed items to camp on their seven-day journey and ten wagons full of food. Gilmos made sure his men could cook which ensured that should the cooks be killed; the men would not starve to death.

Chapter 33:

In the meantime, the enchantress got her seven challenges of monsters ready. "I call upon the lakes and rivers bring to me, the ladies of water, whose songs no man can resist," she said as she called for the first of her monsters, the Sirens She then called upon the seven snaked-headed monsters.

"Oh Great Jungle King who runs through the trees and guards the tablets of destiny, I call upon you and your monkey men for aid in this battle," she said as she called upon the Jungle King, I'Challa

"I call upon the children of Lilith to aide me," she said as she called upon the Lilithian banshees who also lured men to their doom, much like the Sirens.

"Creature of myth born of fire and with the head of a man, body of a lion and dragon's tail, come to me!" Inu chanted, calling upon the manticore that slept within its volcanic lair

"Rats with wings, or so they say, creatures who fear the sun come to me my little ones," she said calling upon the vampires.

"For my final demon, I call upon a demon that is so evil that even the underworld God could not put up with him, Durgess the Dreaded, aid me in my quest!" The enchantress spoke to all the monsters who hated the Gods as much as Inu now did. They hated that their creators whom they loved dearly saw them as mistakes, the Gods, however, were far too kind to kill any of their children because they loved their children, the Gods could not bring themselves to kill any of them. Instead, the Gods sent the heroes of man to erase these creatures time and time again. Yet they always seemed to survive so that their numbers seem to grow again in the darkness of the world. You would think all of them were made by Enlil but that is not the case. It was Tiamat, Goddess of the Seas, who created the mermaids and she had high hopes for them like the fey, but these half-human and half-fish creatures never played that nice. The Sun God Utu had made the manticore, it was said he was trying to help Anu make a lion but added a bit too much fire and so he made a manticore. It was believed that the Banshee was the result of a botched attempt by Anu to make his version of Tiamat's Sirens. Regardless, all of these assembled creatures, the creations of the Gods, failed or otherwise, and so the Gods loved them just as they did their other, more favored creations.

Chapter 34:

On the first day, when they had stopped and rested by a small-large area of cool cold water. The men could hear beautiful singing emanating from the waves. The handmaidens looked at one another and then towards Arwen for to them it was simply a song. Arwen and other women found the soldiers were acting odd to the tune. Arwen saw the men starting to head towards the water as they were in some kind of trance and it seemed even Gilmos was being drawn to the water. To Arwen, the water felt calm and serene and it reminded her of the last time she and Gilmos had stopped here, but she could not help but feel something was off. The water did not seem quite as peaceful as before but was somehow dark and foreboding, rather than cooling and refreshing like before. Even the shade of the water was off for it was a dark teal green rather than its usual cool blue. Arwen saw on a rock several creatures with fish-like tails. These women were half fish and half human beautiful at first glance but had a hidden, sinister nature that it was said no man could resist. Their tails were green, blue, orange, and purple, and their breasts were adorned with seashells, which they wore like bikini tops, and their hair was even decorated with objects from the sea such as clams, and starfish. Arwen's heart stopped for a moment as she saw Gilmos being tempted. She was not certain if this feeling was envy or fear for his well-being. She had heard of these creatures, but had never seen one herself for such creatures did not live where she came from. Mankind had yet to venture beyond what they had known and few who saw these creatures lived to tell the tale, and the ones who spoke of them described them as being beautiful yet deadly and to stay clear of them. The few Sirens that chosen to change their ways could and would love a man but most were monsters bent on the flesh and blood of their prey. They were there to drown and skin the human males that dared to enter their waters. Arwen saw five of the men get close to the creatures and before her eyes; five of the Sirens took on more fish-like features and then prepared to devour the men. Lee and Arwen grabbed three of the men back but did not manage to pull the other two. Sadly, the only thing that remained of those poor souls who had been consumed by the Sirens, was the blood in the waters where they had been standing only moments before the creatures, however, seemed trapped in the waters unable to come to the land. Arwen grabbed several handfuls of moss "I think we can use this, to block the sound," Arwen said as she handed some of the moss to Lee knowing if they did not do something, they soon, they would lose a lot more of the men to these creatures.

"That's a good idea, let's put some in Gilmos ears first," Lee replied. Lee and Arwen filled Gilmos' ears first and headed towards the rest of the men, the other women followed Arwen and Lee's lead and though they lost three more men as they did this they were aware that they could have lost far more if they had not acted quickly. Once their ears had been filled, it took about thirty minutes for them to fully come to their senses. Meanwhile, the Sirens had begun to lose interest in the men because they were not immune to the songs they sung

"My lady, I am sorry I dared look at another woman," Gilmos said, angry with himself for daring to look at another woman, whether he was under a spell or not. "It's fine, I am not the jealous type anyway, besides, who can compete with the Siren's beauty, let alone her song," Arwen replied jokingly

"You should not joke like that for you are far more beautiful than any Siren and far more alluring than her song will ever be and thank you my love for saving my life," he said, kissing her.

"I can't take all the credit; Lee and the other maidens helped me," Arwen said to him.

"Sorry to interrupt, my Lord and Lady, but what's our plan of action? We can't exactly leave these creatures here, they are kind of blocking the path," Lee said.

"Sir we have lost five men total" Xavier interjected

"The cannon, but only enough to either kill or scatter we must conserve ammo for future battles," Gilmos said to his commander. After Xavier had relayed the order to the canon commanders, they opened fire on the Siren, who let out bloodcurdling screams as they scattered. It was hard to tell how many of them were killed, nevertheless, the path was cleared and the army continued. Gilmos knew the enemies would only get tougher as they went and He wondered if he should have brought more men however, he would not ask for reinforcements unless they were needed.

"Xavier, continue to keep track of the casualties, be sure to include their names and ranks that we may honor the fallen when this is concluded." Gilmos ordered

"Understood, my lord," Xavier said. Bowing low before he hurried off to execute his lord's command. Xavier walked around camp to see who was missing. Xavier had come to find the men they lost were some gladiators and some of the cooks. "Sir we have lost three gladiators and two chiefs," Xavier said to the King.

"Lord Gilmos, perhaps as there are no wounded some of us ladies can help with the cooking," Lee suggested

"Very well, let us make camp and hope nothing else comes this night, we should be thankful that this battle took place during the day or we may have found ourselves in a very bad situation," Gilmos said. It was nice to see the King be more heroic and show more his kindness. When Gilmos was around Arwen it was like he was able to show a more loving side instead of the tyrant who had to rule harshly. It was even clear the people had more energy to fight than they did in the past. Arwen noticed Lee was full of happiness seeing the old Gilmos because Arwen seemed to bring that out in him. Arwen fell asleep in the tent next to the King. As she held his hands tightly in hers she realized that she loved him more than anything else in the whole world, what she did not understand, however, that she was afraid to lose him. She knew did not want to lose him to a monster or another woman ever. He was hers and she was his and that was all there was to it. She felt safe and secure when she was near him and her nightmares stopped and everything felt right with the world. He brought out the best in her just like she did him. She brushed his black curly hair before she fell asleep beside him. The next day, after they broke camp and traveled down the path a bit, they would meet up with the seven-headed snake. For this large beast, Gilmos would use the gladiators that remained but what

Arwen and Gilmos did not know was that the blood of these creatures contained a highly potent acid that could eat through flesh and bones in seconds, however, they quickly learned this when one of the gladiator's arms melted off and The second gladiator melted because far too much of the acid fell upon them like a bad chemical reaction.

"At least their heads don't grow back, like myth say," Gilmos said observing that the creature still had five heads remaining. The soldiers used their shields to try and bounce the blood off to buy some time and the handmaidens tried their best to get the acid off quickly. There were not many dead in this battle but several burned from the acid. Three of the handmaids were eaten whole and in one quick swallow. It was at this point that Gilmos decided to send Damien back to retrieve five hundred more men and any woman who would volunteer to be medical aid as well more tools and weapons. They made their camp that night in the trees and on rocks far away from the kill. Gilmos, Arwen, and the rest of the army found themselves rudely awakened by The monkey men who seemed more afraid of the army than the army was of them and it was obvious that the Monkey men did not seem too happy to find humans in their trees. The monkey men were few in numbers.

"Gilmos, I don't think they want us in the trees not to mention they seem to be more scared of us than we are of them," Arwen said motioning for the soldiers to put their weapons down. The monkeys made noise to show they were displeased and even threw bananas at the human intruders. "I suppose just as Tomako was misled; so too were these poor creatures," Gilmos said as he hesitantly lowered his weapon.

"Sir is this wise?" asked Romero.

"I trust Arwen's judgment," he said. The monkeys offered them some bananas as a token of friendship and began to speak in Sign Language, which one of the handmaidens, who was mute, recognized as did another handmaiden, Ella who immediately began to translate:

"They say that the Enchantress hit them and threatened to kill them if they didn't agree to aid her," Ella said.

For what seemed like the hundredth time the Gilmos vowed to kill the Enchantress. He looked at Arwen as if asking her opinion on the matter.

"We should listen to them, maybe an alliance would not be so bad and the reinforcements wouldn't hurt either," Arwen said and as she placed her hand on his shoulder, she told Ella and the Mute to tell the Monkey Men that they were willing to ally with them Gilmos agreed though he was not exactly thrilled with the idea of allying himself with these Monkey Men, Arwen did have a point, they could use the reinforcements

"Sir the woman has lost her mind" Romero whispered in the Kings' ear.

"Maybe…Let's put them in a different area and put three guards on them at night," Gilmos said. In the next battle, which was with the Banshee, Gilmos would lose half of the men and he would learn that the truce with the monkey men would turn out to be a good thing because the Banshee was unable to affect the monkey people. This allowed them to not have a repeat of the Siren incident because Banshees were known to be just as fearsome as the Sirens. After the battle with the Banshees Gilmos, Arwen and their army came face to face with the manticore. Arwen and Gilmos took on the creature together. The manticore was being ridden by a woman who was dressed in black and had her face covered. Gilmos and Arwen wondered if the woman atop the manticore was the enchantress Gilmos drew his sword and tried to stab the manticore, but he missed which caused Gilmos to slip onto the manticore's tail. Arwen let out her wings which Gilmos had not seen until now. He was amazed by how they seemed to sparkle and glitter and had a butterfly look to them. Arwen's wings were an almost pale white color with a hint of purple in them. Arwen swooped down and managed to pick Gilmos up despite the disparity in their masses

"I got this my lady, but thank you for the aid," Gilmos said as she placed him back on the ground

"Stubborn as always, now try not to killed," Arwen said Arwen and Gilmos then tried again to attack the rider and beast. The manticore fought with Gilmos while Arwen attempted to dismount the rider, and once Gilmos had successfully slain the manticore and Arwen successfully dismounted the rider, he or she simply vanished in a puff of smoke. This made Gilmos more certain that the enchantress had shown herself for a moment at least.

The monkey people were deathly afraid of the manticore and with primarily the woman left, the now ragtag group were forced to hide and try and wait for their reinforcements. With the manticore defeated, that left Durgess the Dreaded, Demon of Dreams, whose greatest power was the ability to make feel as though their deepest fears had been realized and the vampires. When the vampires first attacked, the monkeys managed to lure them into the sun. On the second night of the vampire attack, the monkeys had donned the guards' clothes while the humans were hiding underground. Gilmos was hesitant to allow the monkeys to do this but he knew he couldn't afford a full-on battle with the vampires and He trusted Arwen's judgment to trust the fine furry little friends they had made. The monkey men were about half the size of regular humans so they also stacked themselves by threes and twos to seem taller, and when the vampires tried to flee, the monkey men spilled the blood of some of the dead men so the vampires would be compelled by their thirst to feed, and the trap worked so well that the monkey men were able to finish off the vampires quite easily.

After the battle with the vampires, they fought Durgess the Dreaded, who turns out to be the toughest opponent yet, because he seemed to only attack their minds and had no apparent weaknesses and only seemed to attack them when they slept. It was Gilmos who figured out that they could fight back in this "Dreamworld" and when he and Arwen teamed up, they were unstoppable even in this land of dreams. Then the final battle with the Enchantress came, and Arwen and Gilmos hoped that they were ready for it.

Chapter 35:

My, my, you both made it this far, so Anu thinks you two can fight me, Eh? How pathetic. By the time I am dead if you can kill me all my undead will have killed your reinforcements," said Inu. Gilmos and Arwen took up their weapons and Arwen took attacked from the left and Gilmos from the right whilst their soldiers fought some of Inu's undead minions.

"Why is my magic not working?? What could be causing this?" The enchantress said angrily. Gilmos simply pulled out the stone he had been given to disable the enchantress' powers. She grabbed a knife and held the point of it to Arwen's neck.

"Do you I was not going to take what matters to yet again, If I am going down I am taking your treasure great King of Heroes," she said. At the moment Arwen elbowed the Enchantress' ribs as hard as she good, and when Inu let her go she ran beside Gilmos

"I am not a damsel and you are not using me to hurt the King, I will protect him always," Arwen said. Just then five of the monkey men came into the cave accompanied by Anu.

"I will take it from here, my grandson," Anu said. The council of Gods appeared and escorted the enchantress to a prison in a secret place. They offered Gilmos full Godhood but he decided he would stay with his Kingdom and Arwen. The trials the enchantress had sent to tear them asunder only served to make their bond stronger.

Chapter 36:

The Kingdom was saved and Gilmos and Arwen were able to make a life together. The two had a beautiful big wedding and all of the Kingdoms was happy and cheerful and had three beautiful children. Their oldest child was named Hope. Hope had beautiful brown hair and beautiful brown eyes her eyes were much like her fathers. Their next two children were twins Soren Seth, and Lillian. Soren had black hair like his father and Lillian had light purple hair like her mother. The twin's eyes were blue like their mothers. The twins ran into their mother's arm calling out Grandmother and Hope sat in the grass as the wind hit.